"GET THE HELL OUT OF HERE, CAYCE HAMILTON, AND TAKE YOUR UNWANTED OBSERVATIONS WITH YOU!"

Her gray eyes blazed as they impaled Cayce. "Did you hear me?" Shannon stormed in a manner totally out of character for her. "I'm sick of you and your damn meddling in my life . . . sick of Sam Jeffries . . . of all men. In fact, I *hate* men!" Her voice began to wobble. "N-now, not only do I have one idiot after my job, I have you announcing that I'm your fiancée."

The tears slowly spilled over and stole down her face. Shannon watched as Cayce rose to his feet and moved toward her.

"Don't you dare touch me," she cried, stumbling backward to evade his touch. "Don't touch me!"

A CANDLELIGHT ECSTASY ROMANCE®

TEMPESTUOUS CHALLENGE

Eleanor Woods

A CANDLELIGHT ECSTASY ROMANCE ®

Published by
Dell Publishing Co., Inc.
1 Dag Hammarskjold Plaza
New York, New York 10017

Dell ® TM 681510, Dell Publishing Co., Inc.

Candlelight Ecstasy Romance®, 1,203,540, is a registered
trademark of Dell Publishing Co., Inc.,
New York, New York.

ISBN: 0–440–18567–X

Printed in the United States of America
First printing—September 1983

To Our Readers:

We have been delighted with your enthusiastic response to Candlelight Ecstasy Romances®, and we thank you for the interest you have shown in this exciting series.

In the upcoming months we will continue to present the distinctive sensuous love stories you have come to expect only from Ecstasy. We look forward to bringing you many more books from your favorite authors and also the very finest work from new authors of contemporary romantic fiction.

As always, we are striving to present the unique, absorbing love stories that you enjoy most—books that are more than ordinary romance.

Your suggestions and comments are always welcome. Please write to us at the address below.

Sincerely,

The Editors
Candlelight Romances
1 Dag Hammarskjold Plaza
New York, New York 10017

CHAPTER ONE

There was a slight frown creasing the normally smooth forehead of Shannon Bankston as she devoted her entire attention toward getting each word of dictation her boss was throwing out in staccatolike fashion.

She was an expert secretary, capable of taking dictation at a speed far above average, as well as typing eighty to ninety words per minute. Today, however, Cayce Hamilton, well-known personal-injury and criminal lawyer, was madder than ever and taking out his anger on her flaxen head.

A witness, duly summoned, his credibility checked on beforehand, had lied on the witness stand. The changing of his story had caused a delay in a trial that should have gone to the jury at the end of the day.

Cayce, his volatile temper ready to erupt at the slightest provocation, glared at Shannon's slim loveliness, just itching for some sign from her that he was going too fast, perhaps not speaking clearly enough—anything to give him an excuse to vent his rage.

He was a man accustomed to getting his way in both his professional and personal life by out-maneuvering and outthinking his opponents in the legal profession, and by using his considerable charm in dealing with the various women who came and went in his life with the ease of a well-precisioned revolving door.

All except one woman—his legal secretary. Shannon became a challenge from the moment of her first interview for the job. Cayce had taken one look at her slim figure, the perfect, oval beauty of her face framed by the rare color of her hair, and knew there was something different about her.

That difference being—he learned to his regret as their relationship lengthened—her obstinancy, her mulish stubbornness, her temper, not to mention the open disdain with which Shannon appeared to view his life-style.

Cayce bristled under her disapproval. He simply wasn't accustomed to having a woman eye him with such baleful intent or refuse his subtle references toward a more intimate relationship.

8

It didn't take long for Cayce to realize that far from being helpless against his inherent male charm that had allowed him immeasurable conquests, Shannon merely regarded him as a wealthy playboy, likening him to a carousing tomcat, on one heated occasion.

The only time Cayce really had Shannon's full approval was when he was involved in a case. During that period he became a different person. All his attention focused on the defense of his client.

His success was accepted by Cayce without the slightest fanfare. He gave totally of himself and expected the same of others in his employ. He made no apology for his determined drive nor expected any praise. He looked at life in much the same unattached assessment as that of an experienced surgeon cutting with practiced certainty through each layer of skin.

He was a cynic, a realist. He took from life, from each of the affairs he indulged in, never giving of himself, eventually tiring of each woman, and moving on to another. There was something hard and unyielding about him—a combination that seemed to evoke in the women of his acquaintance maternal instincts that were wasted.

The one female who triggered the tiniest spark of emotion in his granitelike makeup showed no interest in him at all.

Socializing between them was limited to occasional working lunches, or a dinner after an exhausting day in court when Shannon accompanied her boss out of town. She had no desire to become another link in the chain of has beens trailing behind Cayce, and steadfastly refused each of his attempts to "deepen" their relationship.

Cayce, his male ego slightly dented after each of their encounters, would be especially testy for a few days, bringing an amused smile to Shannon's lips and in turn a black scowl from her employer.

It was one of those glowering frowns he favored her with now as he prowled around his spacious office, bringing the dictation to an end.

"I see we're not up to our usual standards of proficiency today, Shannon. Did you have a late night? Was Mike Excell more entertaining than usual?" he asked sneeringly, getting a fiendish delight from the barely perceptible tightening of Shannon's lips as she closed the stenographer's pad with a snap, then reached for the two extra pencils she'd placed in readiness on the edge of his desk.

"No more than usual, Mr. Hamilton," she answered crisply as she rose to her feet. "Mike is equally charming and entertaining each time I see him." She met his flinty gaze with her own unrevealing one. "Will that be all?"

"No!" Cayce barked in a gruff fashion, raising one large hand and running his fingers through his hair in a harassed manner. "Are you busy this evening?"

"Well . . ." Shannon hedged. "I do have a few things to do. Do you want me to work late?"

"I suppose you would call it that," he grunted. "Will you have dinner with me?"

"Why?" she bluntly asked.

"Because I need a sounding board. That little escapade in court today left me with a bitter taste in my mouth," Cayce told her with resigned forbearance at her lack of enthusiasm at spending the evening with him. "I'll have you home by ten."

"Sounds fine," Shannon replied, unperturbed by the annoyance in his face. "Do you want these letters to go out today?"

Cayce turned and walked back to his desk and sat down. "In the morning will be fine, Shannon. Why don't you go on home? Perhaps a nice, long soak in a warm tub will enable you to view our dinner engagement on a slightly more pleasurable plane."

"I'm sure Miss Jackson would be only too happy to take my place," she shot back without batting an eye.

They stared at each other across the width of the massive, ornately carved desk, like two unyielding protagonists in a boxing ring. Each recognized in the other an inexplicable something, an affinity that, despite the vast differences in their lives, enabled them to endure the silent war that was always present between them.

Shannon would be the first to admit that theirs wasn't the usual employer–employee relationship. At first she'd tried to maintain a dignified demeanor as she thought befitting her position. But Cayce and

11

his unpredictable personality played havoc with that idea. He wanted a sparring partner, capable of taking dictation, typing without errors, and a sounding board for his various angles in dealing with different cases. Shannon had adjusted her original idea of her duties, thus creating a peculiar rapport between them that would have shocked many of the musty minds in the legal profession.

A secretary wasn't supposed to regard her boss as some sort of lowlife on occasions, yet, she did, and Cayce was vastly amused in the process. She'd learned to shield her expression against suggestions that they spend the weekend at his island retreat or his cabin in the mountains.

She'd also learned to carry on with her work with Cayce perched on the corner of her desk, regaling her with some wild tale guaranteed to send a properly refined secretary scurrying from the room.

Then there were the grueling preparations for a trial, his total dependency on Shannon to see that everything he needed was in his briefcase, nerve-wracking days when he vacillated from a borderline nut to a certifiable maniac. Throughout it all, Shannon hung in, becoming as involved as he in the case, but lacking his innate flair for the dramatic.

"As charming and cooperative as I find Claire to be, and a talent you might do well to copy," Cayce said silkily, "I find that I'm in need of your acid bluntness this evening. You have a way of pointing out my shortcomings with the finesse of a buzz saw."

"Then I'll do as you suggest and leave now. Not possessing the considerable . . . er . . . talents of your latest companion, it will take me quite a while to reduce my inferiority complex to the level that I'll feel comfortable in the presence of such a learned counselor for a dinner companion." After delivering the short speech in her iciest manner, Shannon favored Cayce with the coolest of glacial smiles, then swept from his office, her shoulders erect, her head held proudly.

But even through the closed doors of thick walnut she could hear the uncontrollable laughter that followed her crisp setdown. With a calmness belying the excitement within her, Shannon tidied her desk, made sure the coffeemaker in the small, compact lounge area just off her office was unplugged, the counter tidy.

She came back to her desk, reached for her shoulder bag, and walked out. After a brief conversation with her friend Kitty, the receptionist who had been with Cayce for a number of years, Shannon was on her way.

As she waited for a break in the afternoon traffic, she watched a group of tourists walking past the front of her car, their voices high with excitement as they enthused over various historical points of interest. They were equipped with the usual cameras, guidebooks from the Tourist Information Center clutched in readiness.

St. Augustine was steeped in history, the balmy

13

breezes off the ocean lulling unsuspecting visitors into a drowsy state of contentment that could prove addictive.

Since its beginning, more than one country had laid claim to the coastal city, touted as the oldest in the United States. But throughout it all—the wars, the turmoil, St. Augustine retained its regal bearing, undaunted by the conflict.

Shannon, having lived in Tallahassee most of her life, found the small town of approximately fifteen thousand an enjoyable place to live, the residents friendly.

When she'd first made the move a year ago, she'd done so out of desperation. Shannon had been jilted, painfully and humilatingly so. Jack Treen had been her hero through adolescence, high school, and college. Four years older, and already in law school, Jack had run into Shannon at a party one weekend. Bowled over by the beautiful creature who had emerged from a cocoon of all legs and arms, he'd immediately laid siege to a very willing captive. Three months later he asked Shannon to marry him.

For two years they dreamed and made plans for when Jack would graduate and set up his own practice. By the time Shannon had her degree, the shingle would read TREEN & TREEN, ATTORNEYS AT LAW. Her love for Jack and the eventual attainment of their mutual goals sustained Shannon through the grueling months as she worked part-time for her uncle Cyrus Whittaker and went to college.

The small amount of money left her after her parents' untimely death wasn't enough to see her through college and law school. But with help from her grandmother, with whom she lived, her part-time salary, and her monthly withdrawals against the steadily declining legacy, Shannon managed to scrape by.

She was in her third year of law school when her world exploded into bits and pieces, the shards of grief piercing her cruelly and deeply.

Her grandmother suffered a stroke that memorable summer. Shannon, terrified at the thought of losing her, stayed by her bedside during the critical days. Her only relief was in Jack's visits, his love enabling her to endure the fear of the unknown.

It was during the months of critical convalescence for Amelia Bankston that Shannon began noticing that her fiancé's visits were getting fewer and fewer. Friends who dropped by were careful not to mention his name, puzzling Shannon by their strange behavior as well as the pitying looks they directed toward her.

Cyrus Whittaker dropped by late one afternoon. After visiting with Amelia for a while, he asked Shannon to walk outside with him.

"I don't know of any way to say this other than straight out," he announced as they walked toward the old-fashioned swing hanging from a large oak. "Jack Treen has been offered a position with Grady and Soames"

"Oh, Uncle Cyrus! How wonderful," Shannon exclaimed, reaching out and hugging the graying gentleman with the pencil-slim mustache who had been like a father to her.

"Hmph!" Cyrus snorted, clumsily patting her on the shoulder. "Along with the job, he also gets Pamela Soames. They have been seeing each other behind your back for quite some time now. I've heard their wedding is planned for June—they'll honeymoon in the Bahamas." That was Cyrus's manner—blunt, succinct.

The next day it was Cyrus again who steered a shattered Shannon on another course in her life. An early morning telephone call from him had her in his office that afternoon. She was aware of his coming retirement, but had given little thought to another job. Cyrus, however, hadn't been as lax.

He informed Shannon of her appointment with Cayce Hamilton, an attorney who practiced in St. Augustine, and had even gone so far as to line up a housekeeper-companion for Amelia.

Shannon kept the interview with Cayce, determined beforehand to get the job. She needed the money and the change. His playboy reputation mattered little to her. She was still numb with shock from Jack's careless betrayal. Her only request of Cyrus was his promise not to inform Cayce Hamilton of her personal life, specifically her having been jilted.

She'd dressed conservatively for the interview, the

navy linen suit emphasizing the clean, uncluttered lines of her figure rather than achieving the brisk professional air she'd been aiming for.

Upon being shown into Cayce's office by Kitty, Shannon had absorbed the initial impact of the huge man, who rose to greet her with what she later considered amazing calm. Eyes as blue as the ocean swept her body in leisurely fashion from the top of her head to the tips of her navy pumps.

Shannon later confessed to Kitty that she was certain he'd correctly ascertained her dress, bra, and shoe sizes in that brief space of time. She'd never felt so defenseless in her life, and it angered her. He might be famous for his legal prowess, she'd told herself as she took the chair he indicated, but that didn't give him the right to be so darn brazen.

Her wounds were too new. His blatant masculinity grated on her nerves like the constant throbbing of an aching tooth.

She watched as Cayce returned to the chair behind the desk, unaware that she was conducting her own scrutiny of the intimidating individual before her. The blue eyes were set beneath dark brows that blended in perfect harmony with the craggy features of the deeply tanned face. His nose possessed the slightest hump halfway up its length, the probable result of which Shannon chose not to elaborate upon, considering some of the stories she'd heard.

His air of command was conveyed by the firm thrust of his chin and jaw, as well as the self-commanding set of his broad shoulders. His entire being exuded power and a sexuality that rocked Shannon to the very core of her being. She'd always laughed at such expressions in the past, relegating them to sugary romances and the overactive minds of individuals who authored books on sex.

Now here she was, gaping like a wimp! Even with Cyrus's influence she doubted if Cayce Hamilton would hire her, and she wanted the job. As unobtrusively as possible, Shannon pressed her perspiring palms against her skirt and took a deep breath. By the time Cayce looked up from his perusal of her résumé, her face reflected none of her true emotions. Her expression was one of pleasant thoughtfulness as she waited for him to begin the interview.

"Cyrus mentioned that you are taking some law courses at the university in Jacksonville, night school I believe he said. From what I see here, I'd think you more than qualified as a legal secretary," Cayce remarked, his blue-eyed gaze lingering on her hair in its simple coil at her nape, and the flaxen color.

"Apparently Mr. Whittaker failed to make it clear, Mr. Hamilton. I'm working toward a law degree. I have approximately a year and a half left to go. That is, if I continue to carry my present class load."

Shannon held her breath, silently groaning at this glaring oversight made by Cyrus. Had he been deliberately misleading, knowing how badly she needed the job?

"Am I to understand that you want to be a lawyer?" Cayce asked, an indulgent smile pulling at the corners of his mouth.

His condescending manner caused Shannon to momentarily forget that his hiring her was vitally important to her future. "Not only do I *want* to become a lawyer, Mr. Hamilton, I *will* become one. Due to finances, my plans were temporarily delayed," she quickly informed him. "I do apologize, however, I assumed Uncle Cy—er . . . Mr. Whittaker had explained that I'd only want the job for approximately eighteen months."

Cayce leaned back in the large leather chair and thoughtfully regarded her. "You seem very confident, Miss Bankston. Are you sure you want to pursue a career that's mostly male-dominated?"

"Oh, dear," Shannon warily smiled. "Not you too?"

"Does the question have a familiar ring?"

"Unfortunately yes," she sighed. "I think I must have defended my decision for deciding on a legal career at least a hundred times."

"And you're still determined?" Cayce asked her.

"Absolutely," Shannon replied, her eyes darkening perceptibly at his question. "I'm sure I'll continue to run into the usual die-hards who consider a woman incapable of reading or understanding any written material other than a cookbook, but so far I've managed to defend myself."

"Oh, I'm sure you have," said Cayce, unable to

control the grin that touched his sensuous mouth. "But in defense of my misguided colleagues, let me suggest that perhaps it's your physical attributes that bring out such a reaction. There are those men who are unable to accept brains and beauty in the same package."

"Which is ridiculous. While I've never attempted to capitalize on my looks, I've never downplayed them either."

"No," Cayce shrewdly agreed. "Compromising isn't your style, Miss Bankston, not your style at all. However, my immediate problem is a secretary. Miss White, who's been with me for a number of years, was forced to quit rather abruptly because of ill health." He sat forward, the position of his forearms resting on the edge of the desk causing Shannon's gaze to stray to the broad shoulders beneath the taut material of the jacket of his suit, and to his hands, large and capable, the nails cut close and straight.

"How soon can you start?" he asked. "I refuse to suffer another fool from that damn agency. Besides" —he shrugged and cast Shannon a sheepish grin—"I don't think they have anyone else to send over. I've sent the last three home in a fit of tears. Think you can handle it?"

"What's the salary?" Shannon asked, then almost gasped out loud at the amount he named. "I'll handle it," she said, unable to believe her good fortune.

"There is one aspect that might cause some problems," he added as an afterthought.

"What's that?"

"Occasionally I'll require you to travel with me."

"I see," Shannon murmured, her enthusiasm of only moments ago slightly dipping. There were her night classes to consider. Prolonged or frequent absences would play havoc with her grades. There was also the faint suspicion that Cayce Hamilton just might expect more for his money than a mere secretary. Hurried calculations, however, of her bank account and the months of law school still ahead brought Shannon to a rapid decision. As for any personal problems arising from her new employer, well, she'd handle those, if and when they arose.

"I don't think traveling will be a problem, Mr. Hamilton," Shannon replied far more confidently than she was feeling.

"That's settled then. Can you start in the morning?"

Shannon looked startled. She still had to find an apartment, plus she'd planned on finishing out the week with Uncle Cyrus.

"Is there some problem?" Cayce asked, seemingly perturbed that she hadn't immediately fallen in with his plans.

After explaining her situation, he simply picked up the receiver, flipped open a leather-bound directory on his desk, and began dialing. In less time than she thought possible, Cyrus Whittaker had agreed with Cayce that she was free to start the following morning, or at least to get settled in.

21

The speed with which her immediate future had been settled was most appealing. It would solve a number of problems, the main one being not having to see Jack. Shannon knew he would be out of town for at least three more days.

He'd been so apologetic when he'd informed her of his plans, nothing in his voice or mannerisms betrayed the fact that he was about to dump her. Shannon reddened slightly as she remembered the warm farewell they'd shared, the pride she'd felt as she'd stood and watched her fiancé walk to his car. Yes, indeed, getting away before Jack returned was an unexpected boost to her sagging spirits.

The problem of a place to live was solved by Kitty's offer to let Shannon move in with her, giving Shannon more time to look for a place of her own. Two hours later she was headed back to Tallahassee, her head still swirling from all that had happened.

Now an entire year had gone by, a year of shouting matches, occasionally incredibly long hours, not to mention learning to cope with the steady stream of female admirers that trouped through the doors of the office.

In that year she'd also seen Cayce Hamilton, the defense lawyer, at work. And in spite of her disdain regarding other aspects of his life, he was a master when it came to defending his clients. He possessed the unique ability of persuasion, that gift of believability that was so important in legal defense.

By the same token, he could be ruthless. His razor-sharp mind delighted in tripping up a hostile witness. Once that happened, Cayce would become relentless in his attack. Shannon had watched his performance many times, always more than a little awed by his Machiavellian tactics.

Then there were the occasional moments, such as the incident with the witness earlier in the day, when even Cayce, with all his expertise and cunning, was momentairily stopped by the unpredictability of human failings. A time when his inability to rectify a situation left him restless . . . dissatisfied.

But it never paid to underestimate her boss, she reflected somewhat grimly as she turned into the small parking area to the side of her apartment building. Cayce was noted for striking back in the most vulnerable places. There was a momentary flicker of pity for the witness as Shannon's mind briefly touched on the options open to Cayce.

When she entered the living room of her apartment there was the slightest of pauses in her movements as she let her gaze touch on the cool, comfortable room and its furnishings. She'd been very fortunate in finding this apartment after only two weeks with Kitty, and in the same building as well.

Thanks to the generous salary paid her by Cayce, Shannon was able to occasionally indulge in one of her favorite hobbies—collecting and refinishing old furniture. While all the pieces she'd bought weren't antiques, they were excellent reproductions, adding to the beauty of the high ceiling of the room and the wide plank flooring stained a dark brown.

A large oval braided rug covered the floor in the center of the room, the brilliant colors enhancing the patina of the boards. Unbleached muslin curtains with rust-colored tiebacks complimented the four floor-to-ceiling windows. Her early American sofa was covered in a beige and toast tweed, with accent pillows of rust and orange added for color.

Two wing chairs done in a wheaten background and sprigged with tiny rust-colored flowers completed the focal point.

Shannon dropped her bag and keys on one of the chairs on her way to the bedroom. Before being turned into an apartment, her living room, bedroom, and bath had been one huge sitting room. But careful planning and excellent craftsmanship had resulted in more than adequate sized rooms.

She walked on into the sparsely furnished bedroom, opened the closet, and kicked off her shoes, curling her toes into the thick rug. A sharp glance at the small clock on the table beside her bed showed only an hour and a half before Cayce would arrive.

If she hurried, she could take a quick shower, dress, and get in some studying. She had three exams coming up and needed to spend every spare minute reviewing her notes.

While she undressed and dropped her clothes in

24

the hamper in the bathroom, Shannon wondered what Cayce's reaction would be if she were to call and say she couldn't make it for dinner. "Knowing that unfeeling brute as I do, he'd ignore me," she muttered crossly. She adjusted the shower, then stepped beneath the brisk spray.

Cayce Hamilton had somehow managed to insinuate himself into her life and Shannon wasn't finding it at all pleasant. She didn't want her life complicated at this important time.

Since grammar school, when most of her friends were lost in the fantasy world of seeing themselves as actresses, dancers, or models, Shannon had known she wanted to be a lawyer. The idea had first been voiced out of an inexplicable desire to be different, but in time its appeal grew.

Being on the debating team in high school merely served to reaffirm her decision. A part-time job in Cyrus's law office sealed the idea.

Cyrus was the only male figure in Shannon's life. Her parents had been killed in a boating accident when she was eight years old. But even then her father seemed like a polite stranger. He and her mother were always on the go, parking Shannon with Amelia. Their death, while shocking her with its suddenness, was hardly the wrenching loss of a close-knit family.

As Shannon grew older she accepted the fact that immaturity played a big role in her parents' way of life. A baby had merely been an encumbrance they'd shifted to Amelia, never realizing the treasure they'd so carelessly ignored. Amelia and Uncle Cyrus had been her mainstays.

Looking back, she could see that it had been Cyrus's abrupt ways, his gruff manner that had prepared the way for her to work so well with Cayce Hamilton. They were alike in so many ways, discounting Cayce's varied social life. But, then, she grinned as she soaped one slim thigh, she wasn't sure what Uncle Cyrus had been like in his younger days. There had to be a reason for his having remained a bachelor all these years.

Of the four men in her life, Shannon frowned, Jack and her father, the two who were supposed to have loved her, had left her with a bitter taste in her mouth, an ache in her heart. Uncle Cyrus had remained steadfast, as solid as a rock. Cayce was unsettling, a clear indication, to her way of thinking, that it would be wise to keep a certain distance between them.

Her grandmother and her career were the two most important things in her life, and Shannon intended that it stay that way.

She'd known of Cayce's reputation long before going to work for him, and had been warned by Cyrus to watch her step. A warning she'd laughed off as being ridiculous. She was interested in Cayce Hamilton for two reasons. He was tops in his field, and she knew he paid his staff well. With her own goal almost within her grasp, handling the less admirable side of his personality would be a piece of cake.

Now she realized what an ignoramus she'd been. No woman on the tender side of forty could work day in and day out with Cayce and not become involved. It simply wasn't possible. He was such an exciting and alive person that before one knew it, one was caught up in the swirl of total madness that surrounded him. If one wished to retain her identity, her individuality, as was the case with Shannon, then getting away from him at strategic intervals was vitally important.

His absence from the office between cases afforded Shannon a much-needed respite.

With an irritated toss of her head, she turned off the water and reached for the towel. The brisk rubbing she subjected her body to was done as an unconscious cathartic exercise, the reasoning behind the gesture sensible and well-meaning, the gesture itself futile.

Thirty minutes later, dressed in a white halter-top dress with a softly pleated skirt, her makeup light her hair in its usual neat coil at her nape, Shannon went into the small, compact kitchen and poured herself a glass of iced tea. Armed with the drink, she sat down at the table, drew forward one of the thick textbooks, and began to read.

She became lost in the legal ramifications of con

tracts, only to have her concentration shattered by an impatient pounding on her front door. Masking a muttered oath beneath her breath, Shannon rose to her feet and stalked through the living room, a frown marring her otherwise smooth forehead.

Instead of Cayce arriving early, as she'd feared, it was Kitty, holding a wine cooler, appropriately filled with a bottle of Kitty's favorite, clutched to her chest. "My, my, we are in a bad mood this afternoon," she chortled knowingly, sweeping by her unsmiling hostess with a casual disregard for the fierce glare she was receiving.

"How perceptive," Shannon taunted. She slammed the door and followed her friend into the kitchen. "Are we celebrating something?"

"Friday," Kitty announced airly as she opened a drawer and got out the corkscrew. "Also . . ." The tip of her pink tongue caught between her teeth as she commenced her usual battle with the cork. "Your anniversary."

"How on earth do you manage to keep track of so many dates?" Shannon asked. Kitty came from a large family. Her personal calendar bore innumerable squiggles and marks that only she could decipher. But each member of her family received a card on their special day. When Shannon entered the circle of Kitty's friendship, she was added to the list.

"Who knows?" the pert brunette laughed. "Perhaps it's an identity crisis. With eight children in the family, somebody has to see to such minor details. Now," she stated, pouring the wine into glasses and handing one to Shannon, "let's drink to another successful year to come."

"Correction. Only six more months," Shannon reminded her, then raised the glass to her lips.

"You'll be twenty-five years old and on your own." Kitty shook her head and smiled. "Have you reminded the playboy of the Florida Riviera that you'll be leaving him?" she asked as she drew out a chair and sat down.

"No. But I'm sure there's no need to. Cayce isn't the sort to forget dates. Besides, he won't have any trouble replacing me. I know any number of young women who'd jump at the chance to work for him."

"I suppose you're right," Kitty mused somewhat thoughtfully. "But I would mention it. I have a feeling he isn't going to be so easily pacified when you do leave him."

Shannon wasn't exaggerating about the number of women eager for her job. She would be replaced in less time than she cared to think about. For in spite of Cayce appearing at regular intervals with a different female on his arm, there were those who still cherished the hope of being "the" one.

Not only was Shannon disgusted by the outrageous attempts to snare her boss, she was further appalled by Cayce's total disregard for the feelings of the women who pursued him. His bored acceptance of feminine worship reinforced Shannon's resolve not to become one of the multitude.

But even had Cayce not been such a scoundrel, she would have kept her distance. She'd set goals in her life, goals she was determined to keep. A stopgap love affair didn't figure in her plans at all.

CHAPTER TWO

Kitty's suggestion stayed with Shannon, and during a lull in the conversation, as they gorged themselves on the delicious seafood platter, Shannon glanced at Cayce's roughhewn features.

His expression was unguarded at the moment, leaving her free to take in the familiar planes and curves of his face, the faint signs of fatigue etched so subtly amid the toughness of that impenetrable façade.

She wondered now, as she often had in the past, just why he pushed himself so. For, in addition to his practice, he owned a large cattle ranch in central Florida, where he spent as much time as possible.

It seemed humanly impossible for anyone to go at life the way he did. Relaxation was a word missing from his vocabulary. His idea of relaxing brought a frown to Shannon's face as she thought of his voracious appetite for the supposedly weaker sex.

"Is something wrong with your food?" Cayce's deep voice roused her from her contemplative state with a start.

Shannon met the directness of his blue gaze, quick denial tumbling from her lips. "No . . . no. It's perfect," she assured him. Her hand reached for her glass of wine and raised it to her lips. *Watch it,* a tiny voice inside her whispered, *your tolerance for alcohol is nil . . . if not worse.*

In a gesture of careless disregard of the sensible proddings of her mind, Shannon made considerable inroads into the amber liquid in the stemmed glass. As soon as it touched the linen cloth, Cayce was filling it again.

Afterward he stared at Shannon with a curiously discerning look. "What's on your mind, Shannon?" he asked icily, his biting tone not lost on her.

"Why nothing of great importance, Mr. Hamilton. I was merely wondering how you find time to pursue your hobby with such vigor. I'm surprised you don't keel over from exhaustion," she spoke without batting an eye. Immediately after the words were spoken she wanted nothing more than to sink beneath the table and stay there. *My God!* she wildly thought. *I'm becoming obsessed with his escapades. Why should I care if he sleeps with every woman south of the Mason-Dixon line?*

Instead of the scathing comeback she knew him capable of, Cayce received her colorful comments on his personal life without the slightest flicker of anger. "Perhaps I'm a throwback. I've been told that in his younger days my grandfather was rather fond of the ladies."

"That's a poor legacy to inherit," Shannon observed caustically. "I pity your grandmother."

"Don't," Cayce replied smoothly. "He chose her over all the others. I was also told that he loved her devotedly, and fiercely guarded her." There was an electric pause during which Shannon refused to look up from the food on her plate. "How would you like to be loved like that by one man, Shannon? Would it be possible for a mere mortal to brave that prickly tongue of yours and storm the icy fiord that surrounds your heart?"

By then Shannon knew he was laughing at her. Bolstered by the wine she'd had with Kitty, plus the two glasses with dinner, she raised smoky gray eyes, their depths marked for battle, to his azure blue ones. "Leave my prickly tongue and my ice-laden heart out of this discussion," she ordered imperiously.

"Is that a challenge, Shannon?" He asked the question so softly she could barely hear him over the hum of the other diners.

"Casual affairs don't interest me, Cayce," she snapped, forcing herself to hold his gaze, willing the wild clamor of her heart to cease. "I'd think by now you'd have grown tired of this conversation. We seem to have had it before. Besides, aren't we here to discuss your case?"

He shrugged, a devilish gleam brightening his eyes. "Cases come and go. I'm sure there'll be other disappointments. It's my reputation I'm concerned with. Who knows, I might get lucky one day. I could catch you in a generous mood."

"Oh, you . . ." Shannon couldn't help but grin at his insane teasing. "You're incorrigible. How on earth did Miss White stand you for ten years?"

"Easy. She was twenty years older than me, and got a huge kick out of each of my propositions."

"Speaking of your former secretary, there's a little matter I think I should remind you of," Shannon said, remembering her conversation with Kitty. "You do recall that I'll be leaving in six months, don't you?"

"You definitely are not boosting my sagging spirits, Shannon," Cayce growled, deliberately switching from the relaxed rake to a scowling giant. "To answer your question, I had forgotten—purposely. I've grown accustomed to your . . . er . . . kind ministrations." He eyed her meanly across the table. "Even though I know you regard me as an unscrupulous bastard, it's refreshing to find a female who speaks her mind. I like that. I need a mature woman for a secretary, not a mat I can walk on. That glacial serenity you keep trying to freeze me out with is soothing."

Shannon could do nothing more than stare at his

less than pleased countenance, more than a little amused by his blunt criticism, and at the same time pleased that he needed her. It would be one of those cherished memories she would carry with her when they parted.

"How much would it cost me to get you to change your mind?"

"I beg your pardon?"

"Money, Shannon. The panacea for all problems. How much?" he asked in that concise, outspoken way she'd come to expect.

Rather than being insulted by his question, Shannon was touched. They were poles apart in their thinking, the manner in which they conducted their lives. But there was that indefinable link between them. One that, with the slightest provocation, could catapult them into a collision Shannon knew she'd be a long time recovering from.

She'd met Cayce at a time in her life when his caustic bickering, his outlandish suggestions helped ease the disillusionment of losing the one man she'd thought she loved. He'd bullied her, even taunted her into joining him in his unorthodox routine. The range of their interoffice dialogue was such that Shannon knew she was probably ruined as far as working for anyone else again.

"Well?" Cayce snapped. "Have I finally rendered you speechless? Are you having trouble arriving at a suitable increase in your already exorbitant salary?"

"I don't want any more money, Cayce. You pay

me enough already. But getting that degree is important to me. Surely you can understand that," she softly replied, almost wishing she could give in to the insane whisperings that urged her to stay.

"Yes, damn it, I understand." The sharpness of his voice caused the couple seated at the next table to stare. Cayce shot them a look so quelling, Shannon couldn't help but smile.

"Would you care to finish this discussion at my apartment?" she asked once he'd turned his attention back to her. "I can see that you have very definite views on the subject. I don't know about you, but I find the idea of being the entertainment for the evening very unappealing."

"Aren't you afraid to be alone with me?" he sneered. "I could be seen leaving your place. Doesn't the consequences of such a thing happening cause that ice-laden heart of yours to beat faint from fear of being labeled as one of my women?" he mocked her.

Shannon rested her forearms against the edge of the table, her fingers linked, and stared at him. "My friends would know better. You don't happen to be my type." She delivered the parry with a skilled thrust.

"Touché, Shannon." Cayce nodded in a gesture of defeat. "I concede this round to you. We will, however, continue this vastly informative conversation at your place." He then signaled the waiter for the check.

As they made their way toward the exit, more than one pair of eyes followed their progress. Shannon's flaxen beauty, her quiet poise was a perfect foil for Cayce's dark good looks, the commanding but not overpowering masculinity emanating from his forceful being.

They were almost to the rounded banquette that ran several feet on either side of the double-doored entrance when Shannon looked closer at a group directly in front of her. They were waiting to be shown to a table, and her eyes met the openly admiring stare of Jack Treen!

In a reflexive action that was purely instinctive, she clutched at Cayce's hand, her oval-shaped nails digging into his palm.

"What the hell?" Cayce muttered, staring down at Shannon's face and its alarming pallor, then to the object of her glazed attention.

By then Jack had detached himself from the group and was coming toward them, stopping in front of Shannon, his handsome face bearing a large smile. "Hello, Shannon, what a pleasant surprise," he greeted her warmly, too warmly to suit Cayce, who was viewing the little scenario with grim speculation.

The man's face was familiar, but Cayce was unable to put a name to it. He felt the tremor that shot through Shannon's body, and immediately slipped a protective arm around her waist and drew her against him.

"Hello, Jack," she finally managed through lips

that were stiff in their effort not to tremble. In the silence which was fast becoming embarrassing, Cayce summed up the younger man and found him decidedly lacking, although his curiosity regarding Shannon and this Jack person had him more than a little curious.

He extended his hand perfunctorily, correctly assuming that the clasp of the other man would be limp. "I'm Cayce Hamilton. Your face is familiar, but I can't place your name."

"Jack Treen, sir. I'm with Grady and Soames in Tallahassee. It's really a pleasure meeting you. I've been an admirer of yours for a long time."

"Thank you," Cayce replied in that steely fashion he was famous for, then waited for some indication from Shannon as to the next step. When no such response seemed forthcoming, he took matters into his own capable hands. "If you'll excuse us, we'll be on our way. Give my regards to Grady and Soames." All the while he spoke, he was gently easing the mute Shannon toward the door.

"I'll be happy to," Jack smiled, then reached for Shannon's cold, limp hand hanging at her side and squeezed it. "I hope we'll be seeing each other again, Shannon. Our firm is thinking of opening offices here in St. Augustine. If we do, I'm sure I'll be in charge." He smiled expansively at this announcement.

"How nice for you," she murmured in a quiet voice, firmly removing her hand from his grasp.

Cayce's curt nod of dismissal was such that even

Jack couldn't ignore it. He stepped back, his eyes hungrily following Shannon as she walked away.

Not a word passed between Cayce and Shannon as they walked to the car. One brief glance at her rigid profile was enough to apprise Cayce of the fact that Jack Treen had been more than just a casual friend. There was pain reflected in the pinched features that had the not so surprising effect of causing Cayce to want to do bodily harm to the younger man.

In her own mind Shannon was reliving her own personal torment. On first recognizing Jack, she'd been stunned. It was the first time she'd seen him since Cyrus had informed her of his betrayal.

There was certainly no love left in her heart for the man, but there was still pain at having been used and then tossed aside when a greater opportunity appeared on the horizon.

The giving of one person's love to another was, in Shannon's mind, the ultimate in unselfishness, a gift that was immeasurable. To have that love carelessly trampled on had left scars that only time could heal. She'd departed Tallahassee, leaving behind with Cyrus and her grandmother a sharply worded message for Jack, the general thrust of which was she never wanted to see him again.

Obviously he'd been relieved at not having to face her, his silence hurting almost as much as his betrayal. Shannon knew she'd been lucky in not running into him during the last year.

She couldn't help but wonder if Jack ever regretted

his choice. Pamela Soames was accustomed to getting her way since birth. Would she be content to give up her friends and social status for the slower-paced style of living in the smaller town?

The stopping of the car jolted Shannon out of her unpleasant memories of the past. She looked up and realized they were sitting in front of her apartment. With a sense of dread she turned and looked at Cayce, who was patiently waiting, his enigmatical expression as unreadable as a wall.

"I suppose you're wondering who Jack is." She stated the obvious in a curt voice. Common courtesy decreed some sort of explanation was due him, and Shannon wasn't looking forward to it one bit.

"In a manner of speaking," Cayce replied. "Obviously he's an attorney, and just as obvious is the fact that the two of you were rather close at one time. That's the part I'm curious about. Exactly what was the relationship?"

"We were engaged for two years." She licked her lips and took a deep breath, looking beyond his shoulder into the soft darkness. "He preferred Pamela Soames, plus a partnership in her daddy's firm."

"The slimy bastard!" Cayce growled in a furious tone. "Was that the reason you came to St. Augustine?" he asked her after a brief silence.

Shannon nodded. "I'm afraid I was a coward when it came to staying and wishing the couple well. Cyrus arranged the interview with you, and I didn't argue. I wanted to get away." There was a grimness

40

in her voice that wasn't lost on Cayce as he listened and watched.

He was seeing a vulnerability in his redoubtable Miss Bankston, gaining an insight into the reason behind that wistfulness, the hint of sadness he'd seen reflected in her eyes from time to time.

"Did you love him?" Cayce asked gruffily.

Shannon looked sharply at him. "Of course I did. We were engaged. I'd had a crush on him from the time I was twelve years old."

"Then why didn't you stay and fight for him? If you loved him as much as you say, wasn't he worth the effort?"

"It wasn't that simple," Shannon defended her decision. "I had a grandmother who was recuperating from a stroke. I was trying to go to school as well as work." She shook her head. "At the time I only wanted to get away. I felt betrayed and I was hurt. I couldn't afford the luxury of taking my time, of thinking rationally," she argued.

"Rational thinking has nothing to do with it, Shannon," he pointed out with impatience. "I think if you had really loved him, you'd have found a way. It seems more a case of hero worship than love."

"Just how would you know?" she threw the question at him. "You've never stayed with the same woman long enough even to learn her choice in food, let alone to recognize real love." She glared furiously at him.

"Ahhh." Cayce sounded almost gleeful as he rested one long arm on the steering wheel and leaned toward her. "Now we're getting somewhere. But as usual, Miss Prim, you're trying to change the subject to my—what you consider to be—decadent, debauched style of living, aren't you?" When Shannon was forced to let her gaze drop, he continued. "You've let that limp-handed son of a bitch sour you on ever enjoying a normal, healthy relationship with a man."

"Such as you, I suppose!" Shannon flared, then blushed to the roots of her flaxen hair. *He's such an egotistical ass,* she thought angrily. *I wish I'd never even attempted to explain.*

Cayce leaned back, a mischievous grin curving the attractive line of his sensuous lips. "For once, Shannon, I agree wholeheartedly. An affair with me would not only bring a glow to those smoky eyes, it would totally expunge from your mind all thoughts of Jack Treen. I'd see to that."

Shannon took a firm grip on her rising temper, her fists tightly clenched. "Thank you, Mr. Hamilton. I appreciate your generous offer. I do hope you'll forgive me though if I don't accept. I'm afraid of being trampled by the stampede of women from twenty to fifty!" she yelled the last part at him, then wrenched open the door and got out.

With ill-concealed grace she stalked up the bricked walkway, muttering imprecations upon Cayce's dark head. He possessed the morals of a guttersnipe! He had no qualms about equating each sensitive, tender emotion with his own selfish philandering, to which there could be no comparison.

What she'd experienced with Jack had been special. Something beautiful, regardless of Cayce's cynical views. Up and until the day she learned she'd been betrayed, she couldn't have been happier. Their shared moments, their dreams were wonderful and real. Cayce couldn't began to understand such a relationship. How could he? A prerequisite for sensitivity and love between two people required that both parties have warm, beating hearts. Cayce functioned like a machine, with water in his veins!

In her anger Shannon hadn't bothered checking on Cayce's whereabouts. It was only as she entered the foyer that she became aware of him close behind her. She turned and glared at him. "I take back the offer of coffee, Mr. Hamilton," she informed him in a nasty little voice. "I would prefer to be alone."

"And I would prefer that you not be, Shannon," he said silkily. "Your gimlet-eyed Jack isn't worth the buckets of tears you'll shed over him if left on your own."

"I've no intention of crying over Jack. I got that out of my system a year ago." She spoke tersely as she inserted her key into the lock and opened the door to the softly lit room.

"I'm glad to hear it. We can enjoy our coffee while I continue to try to bribe you into not leaving me." He brushed by her, loosening his tie and removing it and his jacket on the way to the sofa. Both articles of clothing were tossed toward a chair while he dropped in a relaxed sprawl on the sofa.

Shannon regarded him through narrowed eyes, her lips grimly pursed. "I'm really not in the mood for company," she reminded him.

"That's too bad, because I am—yours. In case you've forgotten, I suffered a major setback in court this morning," he announced piously. "It's part of your duties as my personal, private secretary to help me adjust to that inconvenience," he informed her without batting an eye as she continued to regard him.

"Why not go see Claire Jackson? Considering the amount of money you've spent on flowers, not to mention that beautiful bracelet, I'd think she would be more than happy to entertain you for a while."

"Oh, she would be. Claire is a very . . . er . . . affectionate person," he remarked with studied casualness, grinning at the twin dots of red that appeared on Shannon's checks. "She's quite innovative in her repertoire of little things that please a man. You should talk to her sometime; it could prove useful in the future in keeping your men from straying."

"Why you—you—oooh!" she stammered stormily, then whirled around and rushed from the room. In the kitchen each step in preparing the coffee he'd insisted on was punctuated by a series of slamming doors and the total disregard for her china as cups and saucers were unceremoniously thumped against the tray.

"Men!" she angrily muttered, damning the entire lot of them. She was convinced the only way for a woman to survive in their chauvinistic world was to keep all members of the opposite sex at a healthy distance. Jack had proved as faithless as a snowball in an oven, and Cayce was only interested in his own egotistical self, not to mention his considerable sexual appetite! *I'll show them,* she silently vowed as she leaned against the edge of the counter, her arms crossed in front of her. *I'll show them both.*

By the time the coffee was ready, Shannon had managed to cool down. She was used to Cayce's goading, his deliberate attempts to shock her. If she were honest with herself, she'd admit that his brisk handling of Jack's sudden appearance as well as his forcing his company on her *had* kept her from crying over what might have been.

Shannon sighed as she added sugar and cream to the tray. Cayce might possess qualities she found abhorrent. He *was* pushy and overbearing. But in his own callous way he'd offered her a way out of a miserable few minutes, even to the point of allowing her to keep her pride intact. It was yet another look into the complex nature of the man who had dominated her life for the past year.

How was it possible for such a man to have sympathy and understanding on one hand, when he made no attempt in his own life to remain faithful to any one woman? *But therein lies the difference,* the tiny voice within Shannon whispered. *Cayce makes no promises, draws the line at commitments. He admits to being a rake, and makes no apology for it. A woman foolish enough to cast her lot with him knows from the beginning that the relationship will be of a short duration.*

As she entered the living room bearing the tray, Shannon saw that her guest had apparently tired of waiting and was prowling about the room, his hands thrust finger-deep in the waistband of his trousers.

"Impatient, Mr. Hamilton?" she asked coolly, setting the tray on the coffee table, then seating herself on the sofa and filling each cup with the aromatic brew. "Does Miss Jackson have some super-quick way in which she prepares coffee that I should know about?" she asked maliciously.

Cayce turned and stared at her through slitted lids before speaking. "Get a hold on that damnable temper, Shannon. I'm in no mood for your barbed tongue." He crossed the room in a lazy gait that barely concealed the latent force of his huge frame.

"I would like to point out, before I'm banished to silence, that you did invite yourself." Shannon smiled frostily at him as he dropped down uncomfortably close beside her. Without thinking, she added two spoons of sugar to his coffee and handed it to him.

"A fact I'm beginning to question the wisdom of," he scowlingly admitted, idly stirring the hot drink.

Shannon became uneasy in the silence that followed. After a while she risked a cautious look in his direction, surprised to find him staring broodingly at her. She swung her gaze back to the cup she was holding, suddenly finding herself shy of this large, intimidating person sharing her sofa.

"Was he your lover?" The question caught her by surprise, the tone of his voice chilling her with its iciness.

Shannon kept her eyes on the contents of her cup, seeming inordinately fascinated by some mysterious findings in the dark depth. What right did he have to question her? What business was it of his if she'd slept with ten men or twenty men? "Isn't that rather personal?" she asked in muttered embarrassment.

"Was he?" Cayce persisted in his deadliest cross-examining voice. Shannon had heard that timbre, that single-mindedness behind a question, too many times to harbor any hopes of deterring him.

She set her coffee down on the table and then let her body slump back against the cushioned softness of the sofa. "Yes." She uttered the one word of admission defeatedly. "Do you find it so difficult to believe that I too could be swept up in the throes of passion?" she asked bitterly, staring unseeingly at the ceiling.

"Not at all," Cayce drawled. "I'm only sorry that you wasted that first burst of youthful passion on such an unscrupulous bastard as Jack Treen. It's obvious by his cowardly actions that he wasn't man enough to appreciate the precious gift he'd been given."

Shannon was stunned by his reaction. She'd expected ridicule, even mockery, but never in her wildest dreams had she considered that he'd be in any way understanding. She took so long assimilating this shocking turn of events that Cayce became restless.

"Did you think I'd be happy to learn you'd been humiliated? That you'd had your pride trampled on?" he asked gruffly. He placed his cup beside hers on the table, then reached for her, his long arms drawing her against the warmth of his body for the second time that evening.

Shannon stiffened at this proprietary gesture. She much preferred Cayce in his usual role of blunt employer rather than that of comforter. She moved as though to pull away, only to be told in a succinct voice to "Stop squirming."

With as much calm as she could manage, Shannon did as she was instructed, trying to ignore the curious pounding of her heart. "Is this supposed to be lesson number one in my education you spoke of earlier? Or are you perhaps thinking that I'll fall victim to Jack's charms again?" she asked in an attempt at sophisticated banter. Instead, it came over as harsh, indicative to someone as discerning as Cayce, of the real hurt within her.

"If I thought that, my dear Shannon, I'd resort to measures that would shatter that frigid little heart of yours into a thousand pieces. Think of this as purely spontaneous. Two people enjoying a pleasant evening—nothing more. Unless . . . that is"—one large hand fit itself beneath her chin and forced her head up—"you'd care to know what it's like to be made love to by a man instead of a sweaty-palmed boy."

Shannon stared incredulously into his blue orbs, outraged by his blatant suggestion. "Why, you unscrupulous fink . . . you egotistical ba—"

Her furious spate was abruptly halted by Cayce's covering her mouth with his. Suddenly she was filled with a fear that caused her to struggle in earnest against the twin fetters of steel that held her. Her mind shrieked out its warnings of impending disaster if she allowed this situation to continue. But instead of being content with the same impassiveness he'd accepted in the past, Cayce was now determined, demanding in his deliberately provocative assault on her lips.

His tongue traced the tender outline in protracted leisure, even as he effectively halted each attempt of hers to wrench free of his arms. Finally tiring of the stubborn clench of her teeth against any further invasion, Cayce slightly shifted their bodies so that one of his hands was free to idly caress the proud thrust of Shannon's small, firm breasts through the silky material of her dress, finding and stroking first one erect tip and then the other.

As expected, Shannon opened her mouth to protest this intrusion and Cayce took full advantage, plunging his tongue into the moist, excited warmth of her mouth. In a trembling moan of acquiescence she knew the battle was lost. With the combined efforts of his hands, exacting the most heavenly sensations of pleasure from one part of her body to his tongue, challenging her to meet each of his plundering thrusts, she was lost in the urgency that was sweeping over her. An urgency that not only smashed the barrier of her resistance, but carried slim arms to encircle his neck, her fingers losing themselves in the thickness of his dark hair. She reveled in the crisp springiness that had so often intrigued her, wondering how it would feel.

Her only coherent thought in the maelstrom of Cayce's lovemaking was that he was as aroused as she, for whatever comfort that might be later on.

When Cayce forsook the now swollen sweetness of her lips to blaze a fiery trail along the slender column of her neck, and lower to the dusky shadow between her breasts, Shannon offered no protest. It was as though she were obeying the edicts of some presaged happening, powerless to control or interrupt or stop the turn of events. She was a helpless victim until the pendulum had swung full circle.

There was no further surprise or shock when she felt her back press against the cushioned seat of the sofa, nor at the release of the single fastener that secured the haltered bodice at her nape. Its flimsy protection was brushed aside, baring the burgeoning fullness of her breasts to his burning gaze, his questing hands.

She opened smoky gray eyes—their mirrored depths glowing like luminous pools—to meet the startling blue gaze that was staring, not in triumphant anticipation as she'd imagined, but broodingly . . . almost . . . Shannon let her eyes slowly close to blot out that disturbing look.

With a muffled groan Cayce paid homage to the pink-tipped loveliness before him, his lips gently laving each nipple until Shannon was arching against him, urging him on with complete abandonment of her former strict rules regarding Cayce Hamilton!

In the feverish turning of her head, the neat coil at her nape came undone, the heavy fullness of her hair tumbling unrestrained about her face and shoulders. Cayce ran his hands through the silken strands, then buried his face in its scented thickness.

"My God!" he whispered against Shannon's neck, his voice harsh against the ethereal quiet that surrounded them. "You're beautiful."

Shannon tried to dismiss the sound of his voice from her mind, not wanting to engage in conversation. She had no words to offer—wanted no exchange of frivolous nothings. Her body was clamoring for release, for an ending of the tortured flames of desire lashing out at her.

"Open your eyes, Shannon," Cayce gently demanded of her. When she stubbornly held on to the slowly diminishing passion that bound them, Cayce touched her face, cupping her cheek with his palm. "Look at me," he demanded, forcing her to obey him.

With a sense of dread that tore at her insides, Shannon met his gaze, uncaring that her eyes, her face, her entire being, was as easily read as block letters standing ten feet tall. "Why?" she whispered.

"Because I want you to be fully aware of what I'm about to say."

"And if I choose not to listen?" she asked, unwittingly provocative in her response.

"You will, honey, you will. I'll see to it," he grimly retorted. With a completely unexpected move he caught the two straps of her dress and fastened them, letting one hand slide down to rest against her now covered breasts. "You do know what will happen here and now if we don't stop, don't you?"

Shannon turned her head and stared at the back of the sofa, reality bringing with it the ultimate in humilation. She wanted nothing more than to crawl into a hole and die.

It wasn't the knowledge that she'd lost her head. She was a normal, healthy individual, with no hangups regarding sex. But with Cayce Hamilton? The unprecedented tomcat of all time? *I cannot, I simply cannot face him,* she inwardly groaned. With the heavy curtain of her hair shielding her face, Shannon pushed herself into a sitting position, pressing close against the opposite end of the sofa.

"It won't do you any good to pretend I'm not here, Shannon." Cayce broke into her embarrassed thoughts, amusement plainly evident in his lazy drawl. He reached out and slid a hand beneath her hair, his fingers lightly caressing the heated smoothness of her neck. "Are you angry because I didn't make love to you?" he asked in that teasing, taunting way she hated.

"No!" she exclaimed, swinging round to stare at him, the swollen softness of her lips, the rosy glow of her features attesting to the extent of her passion. "Don't be ridiculous, Cayce." She weathered his knowing look with bluffed composure. "We simply got carried away. We're both consenting adults, nobody was hurt, so just let it drop."

"What if I choose not to let it drop? What then?" he asked lazily, reminding Shannon of a cat teasing a cowering mouse.

"Then I'm afraid for once in that pampered life of yours you'll have to. I have no intention of having an affair with you, or acting as a convenient substitute when your current flame is unavailable," she snapped, refusing to be swayed by the wave of pure sexuality emanating from him. Even in her anger she was startled by his power to excite her.

Her gaze slid from the dark hair she'd caressed and his roughhewn features that were indelibly stamped in the mirrors of her mind to the crisp hair covering his chest that was visible where the front of his shirt was open. She remembered the rock-hard muscles of his shoulders, could see the trim waist, the flat tautness of stomach and thighs.

Oh, yes, she was forced to admit silently, *you are the king of the playboys! Even after one very minor skirmish with you I'll have a wealth of memories. An affair would destroy me.*

"Good night, Shannon." Cayce broke the spell holding her in its compelling grip. With infinite tenderness he leaned over and dropped a light kiss on her lips. "I repeat . . . Jack Treen is a damned fool."

Shannon made no effort to play the role of the perfect hostess. She watched with a strange detachment as Cayce retrieved his coat and tie, hooking both with one long forefinger and slinging them over his shoulder. He paused at the door and turned, looking back at her, the most enchanting smile she'd ever seen coming to his lips, as he softly whispered "Sweet dreams, princess."

When the door closed on his disturbing presence, Shannon exhaled raggedly. She'd always recognized a primitive danger in Cayce. That accounted for the cool, impenetrable wall—or so she thought—she'd erected against him.

She reached for one of the rust-colored pillows and clasped it to her chest, her face mirroring the dismay she felt. She been helplessly duped by one man, her easy accessibility pointed out with unqualified success by another. At the moment, she knew the recovering of her pride would be painful, excruciatingly so. But she would recover, and the Jack Treens and the Cayce Hamiltons of the future could take notice. Shannon Bankston would emerge a formidable adversary.

CHAPTER THREE

Shannon sat at her desk and stared moodily at the file spread out before her. It was happening again, she sighed, as she sought to focus her thoughts on the work at hand, and away from the haunting face of Cayce Hamilton.

She leaned back in her chair, resting her head against the tall, leather-covered back, a mixture of emotions flickering across the classical features of her face. It had been six months now since she'd left Cayce. Months in which there'd been a degree of happiness and personal satisfaction in that she'd graduated from law school, and was now associated with a prestigious firm.

So why can't I stop the past from intruding, she asked, then immediately chided herself for being so silly. Whether or not she liked it, Cayce Hamilton was still in her thoughts, her dreams, and probably would be for a long time to come. Quite simply, Shannon missed the arrogant, overbearing brute.

In the calmer moments of rational thinking, she would congratulate herself on the progress in her career, looking upon the time spent with Cayce as that of an apprentice learning the trade from the expert. But invariably she was forced to admit that, though she'd won the war in accomplishing her goal without Cayce around, the victory was far from sweet.

Her thoughts went back to that night in her apartment almost a year ago, when she'd fallen so easily beneath his spell. The ensuing six months had become a day-by-day battle of wills as Cayce became more fractious, more demanding. It seemed to Shannon at the time that he was punishing her for even thinking of leaving him.

Only she knew how difficult some of those months had been. She even found herself unable to understand the sense of regret that nagged at her. There'd been agonizing moments after she left when she had to clench her fists to keep from picking up the phone and calling Cayce, the need to hear the deep gravely timbre of his voice like an incurable ache in her chest.

She even, for one brief moment, became fascinated by any man with blue eyes, always looking for that particular, brilliant shade that was stamped in her memory.

Worst of all had been the loss of his touch, albeit impersonal . . . helping her from a car, an arm slung casually about her shoulders as they left the courtroom, little things that had crept unnoticed into her store of memories and refused to be replaced by mere changes in address or position.

Oh, yes, if Cayce had known how attracted to him she really was, how difficult it had been to leave him, Shannon was sure he would have danced a jig of glee.

And yet, that one time he'd had her at his mercy, he'd acted completely out of character. Part of her had been grateful, the other part chafing at how easily he'd halted their lovemaking.

That last day as his secretary and the bitter words that passed between them floated before her mind's eye. Shannon had offered a stiff speech of how it had been a pleasure working for him. Cayce had sat behind his desk, unmoving, those blue eyes mercilessly raking her slimness as he listened. After she'd finished, a brief smile, so devoid of emotion that it chilled her, touched his mouth. "Spoken like the excellent employee you've been, Shannon. However, you will forgive me if I don't believe you, won't you? There's hardly a day gone by that you haven't hated my very guts. Only two things kept you here . . . and we both know what they are. My experience and the attractive salary. Any other trumped-up reasons would be an insult to us both."

Shannon stood trembling before him, knowing he spoke the truth. And yet there was that intangible something between them that was impossible to grasp. "I'm sorry we have to part enemies, Cayce. I'd like to think of you as my friend." Her gray eyes begged for understanding.

There was the briefest narrowing of his gaze as he continued to regard her. "We'll never be friends, Shannon, so put that ridiculous notion out of your mind. Save such soppy thoughts for the likes of Jack Treen."

The ridicule in his tone and his thoughtless reference to Jack stemmed all her efforts of friendliness toward him. "You are without a doubt the most hateful person I've ever known, Cayce Hamilton. Why don't you stop and take a really good look at your life? You're thirty-seven years old, with no one to care if you live or die. The women you sleep with are interested only in one thing—your bank account. You scoff at every decent emotion, too cowardly to really face life and its challenges. Well, you're right about one thing"—she leaned forward on the desk, her clenched fists supporting her body—"I'm glad to be getting away from you!" She turned on her heel and stormed from the room before the tears that had been gathering in her eyes could spill over.

Her only other communication with Cayce during the last six months had been in the form of a card at graduation, with a nice fat check tucked inside. Shannon wrote a simple thank-you note, and deposited the check. The unexpected death of her grandmother had brought a handwritten missive, expressing his condolences and his regret that he'd been away and unable to attend the funeral. The sincere wording had touched her deeper than she cared to admit.

The sharp buzzing of the intercom brought Shannon out of her disturbing reverie. She sat forward and depressed the button. "Yes, Maria?"

"There's a Miss Kitty Lang to see you, Miss Bankston. Shall I send her in?"

"Of course, Maria," Shannon replied excitedly, a huge smile brightening her face. She pushed back her chair and rose to her feet. Just as she came around her desk, the door to her office burst open.

"Miss Bankston? Of the firm Hardwicke, Granville, and Granville?" the vivacious brunette questioned. "The famous lawyer?" She then promptly dissolved into helpless laughter as she met Shannon in the center of the room, their arms going around each other, their voices raised in excited greeting.

"Be serious now and let me look at you," Kitty instructed in mock sternness after the emotional excitement had died down, her sharp gaze taking in the gradual loss of weight that had eaten away at Shannon. "Good heavens! Don't they allow you time out to eat in this place?" she exclaimed, not at all pleased with the lack of sparkle in her friend's eyes, the evident signs of fatigue etched in the delicate features of her face.

"They do, but when you're trying to prove yourself, sweetie, you tend to let less important things

60

slide," Shannon ruefully explained, waving her friend to one of the chairs positioned in front of her desk.

"Less important, eh? Like eating three square meals a day, not to mention getting a proper night's sleep once in a while."

"All right, you frustrated mother hen. So I'm not up to my usual fabulous self. Stop fussing and tell me what you're doing in Jacksonville." She skillfully steered the conversation from her appearance to a more interesting topic. "Are you indulging in one of your famous shopping sprees?"

"In a manner of speaking," Kitty airly replied, her eyes alight with a devilish gleam. She tilted her curly head at a saucy angle and inspected the perfect oval of her pink-tipped nails in an infuriatingly bored manner. "I'm overseeing the setting up of a law office. I'm also looking for an apartment for myself. Any suggestions?" Her eyes danced as she regarded Shannon, who was sitting on the corner of her desk.

"You've left Cayce?" Shannon asked in a shocked voice. She stared at her friend as though she had suddenly taken leave of her senses.

"Not exactly," Kitty said, determined to play out the mystery to the very end. "Aren't you pleased that I'll be close again? It's really been lonesome with you gone. I've missed our impromptu wine parties, not to mention being glared at by the hostile old maid who took your apartment."

"Look who's calling who an old maid," Shannon

scoffed good-naturedly. "You and I are fast approaching that not-so-glamorous period in our own lives. But seriously, have you left Cayce?"

"All right," Kitty sighed. "I suppose I'll have to confess. Cayce is relocating his office. For some strange reason he suddenly decided he preferred being in the thick of things. He could just as easily practice in a boat. The type of client he attracts will seek him out, regardless of where he goes. By the end of the week we should be settled in."

"I see." Shannon spoke softly, the news leaving her with a peculiar sense of impending doom, which was ridiculous, she scolded herself. Cayce Hamilton was no longer a part of her life. Why should she care where he chose to practice?

"Shannon? Does the idea bother you? Knowing Cayce will be so close, I mean?" Kitty asked. She wasn't a fool. In the last six months that Shannon had worked for Cayce, she'd seen the strain between them, the forced politeness, the effects of which often had Shannon ready to pull out her hair by the end of the day.

"No, of course not. I'm just surprised, that's all. As you said, his speciality allows him almost carte blanche as far as locations go." She gave Kitty a curious half smile. "It is puzzling though. I thought he enjoyed the quietness of St. Augustine."

"Well, since I wasn't consulted, I can't really shed any light on the subject. There is, however, my own problem of a place to live. Any suggestions?"

Shannon stared at Kitty, an idea beginning to take root in her mind. "How would you like to move in with me? It's the least I can do, considering my imposition on you when I first worked for Cayce. Like you, I was desperate for a place when I arrived here. The only decent apartment I could find, other than an efficiency, had two bedrooms. The rent's outrageous, but the benefits are super."

After only a moment's hesitation Kitty accepted. "Exactly what do the super benefits consist of?" she asked pertly.

"Men—droves of them—as well as the usual swimming pool, tennis courts, sauna, and topnotch security. There's even a fireplace. Of course, with our weather, we won't be able to use it much, but it does add a nice touch."

"You, my dear, are now the possessor of a room-mate. Figure out my share of the expenses and I'll write you a check," Kitty briskly ordered. "We'll alternate weeks getting dinner." Then she frowned. "On second thought, I think I'd better take over the kitchen. You don't seem to be doing so hot in that department."

"Your wish is my command." Shannon laughed at how quickly Kitty was taking over. It would be a refreshing change having her around. Kitty often reminded Shannon of a small tornado. It would also be a relief not to have to come home to an empty apartment night after night. Work had its good points, but a steady diet had the strange affect of causing one to lose sight of reality.

"When will you be moving in?"

"Is tomorrow okay?"

"Sounds great. Here." Shannon stood, then walked behind her desk and reached into a drawer for her purse. "Take this extra key. But let's don't forget to get another one from the manager." She grinned. "I've been known to misplace mine."

"How well I remember," Kitty laughed. "It was always when I was sleeping soundest." She glanced at her watch, then back to Shannon. "Can you have lunch with me?"

Shannon looked at the stack of work on her desk, knowing if she did, she'd have to stay late. But what the heck? "Sure. I haven't taken a decent lunch break in ages." She picked up her purse. "Let's go."

Sometime later, replete after a chef's salad and a huge slice of pie, Shannon sat back contentedly in her chair and regarded her friend. "I can't tell you how good this is, the two of us laughing—gossiping. I've really missed it."

Kitty swallowed the sip of coffee she'd just taken. "Why are you pushing yourself so hard, honey?" she asked. "I know you have friends here, I've met some of them. Yet, each time we've talked, even today, I get the impression that you've cut yourself off from everyone. Is that a prerequisite for achieving success or are you having problems?"

"A little of both, I suppose," Shannon confessed,

surprised to find that she needed to talk to someone. She felt as though she'd been marooned on some desert island for the last few months instead of starting out in a career she'd worked so hard for.

"You have no idea how difficult it is proving that you're a lawyer first, a woman second. I even have to watch the way I dress." She shrugged. "There are times when I'd like nothing better than to put on my sexiest dress, leave my hair down, and watch their eyes pop out. I'm sure it would set me back as far as ever being taken seriously, but it would almost be worth it to rattle their chauvinistic minds."

"How do the members of the firm treat you?" Kitty asked curiously. She knew the question would keep Shannon talking, which was exactly what was needed.

"Actually they're very supportive, except for one of the junior members. And I'm beginning to be trusted with very small, but not very complicated cases. Before that I thought I'd never get out of the library. I've developed a hearty dislike for extensive research."

"But do you like it? Are you finding it as fulfilling as you imagined during all those years of school?"

"Yes," Shannon answered unhesitatingly. "Right now I know I don't sound like it, but each day it gets a little easier." She grinned. "I suppose after being around Cayce I envisioned myself strutting about the courtroom in a blaze of glory, dazzling everyone with my brilliance." She sighed. "Unfortunately it takes considerable time and experience before one achieves his enviable status."

"He is something to see, isn't he?" Kitty murmured. After Shannon's departure she'd been forced on several occasions to fill in as Cayce's secretary, a position she found to be absolutely terrifying. But however difficult she found the man himself to be, she could find no fault with his legal prowess.

"He's the best. That's the reason I couldn't accept the position he offered me as his associate. I'd always feel I was an extension of his ideas, his thoughts. He's so overpowering, one tends to lose one's identity." She spoke musingly.

"Is that the reason for the chill in the air the last few months you were there?" Kitty posed the question lightly, a picture beginning to form in her mind.

"Partly. I don't think he's forgiven me for refusing. How's his present secretary working out? I remember your saying he'd gone through four in three months."

"Please!" Kitty held up one hand in a staving-off gesture. "I thought I would go stark raving mad before I found Mrs. Kite. She's in her early fifties, and a paragon among secretaries. Since her arrival on the scene I can go to work without fear of being called into the lion's lair. I swear, Shannon, I don't know how you did it."

Shannon laughed at the distress mirrored in Kitty's face, relaxing as the conversation drifted from one thing to another. By the time they parted outside the restaurant, she was even more convinced that she'd done the right thing in asking Kitty to move in with her.

All during the afternoon, as she consulted countless tomes for precedents in the case she was researching, Shannon was unable to erase Cayce from her thoughts. He was coming to Jacksonville, and she had no idea what his motives were for the move.

Instead of working till nine thirty or ten o'clock as had become a habit, Shannon called it quits shortly after seven. The slightly nagging pain in her temples that had been present when she first awoke that morning had now blossomed into a raging headache. Kitty had also called and said there was a chance she would drop by with some of her clothes. Even though Kitty had her own key, Shannon wanted to be there if she did come by.

She pushed back her chair and stood, quickly gathering up her pen and legal pad, sliding both into her slim leather briefcase. After returning the heavy volumes to their rightful place in the bookcase, she walked across the room, turned off the light, and closed the door.

Several minutes later found her seated behind the wheel of her ancient Volkswagen as she tried to concentrate on the traffic and ignore the excruciating pain in her head.

As soon as she reached her apartment, Shannon went straight to the bathroom and the the cabinet where she kept the aspirin. After shaking two tablets from the bottle, she filled a paper cup with water and swallowed the medicine.

With a weary sense of—she wasn't sure what—something gnawing at her, Shannon began to undress, dropping her blouse and lacy underwear into the wicker hamper, then carried her skirt and blazer back into her bedroom.

Instead of taking the shower she was longing for, she decided to give Kitty another hour. *In the meantime,* she told herself, *I'll fix a cup of tea and try to go over my notes.* Sam Jeffries, with whom she was working on the Bramlett case, would like nothing better than to find some fault with her research.

He was one of those egotistical nerds who considered a woman incapable of anything other than having babies and being a housekeeper. Shannon had had more than one run-in with him since joining the defense firm of Hardwicke, Granville, and Granville.

There were four junior members, including herself, as well as the three founders. Messrs. Granville and Mr. Hardwicke were remarkably liberal in their thinking, and had gone out of their way to make Shannon welcome, as had Jim Blalock and Chris Yancey. They each tried to shield her from Sam Jeffries. But in Shannon he'd found more than he bargained for.

She'd struggled too long and hard to allow the likes of Jeffries to deter her in her climb to the top. Since her arrival, the hallowed walls of the old firm had been privy to a number of clashes between the newest member and Mr. Jeffries!

There was a comfortable silence in the cozy living room, the only light coming from the lamp at one end of the sofa, where Shannon was sitting, her legs crossed in a lotus position as she studied her scribblings on the legal pad.

Suddenly the quietness was shattered by two sharp rings of the doorbell. In a graceful move Shannon came to her feet and hurried to the door, tightening the belt of her emerald green robe as she went.

Instead of her usual precaution of asking who the caller was, she flung open the door, a smile of welcome on her face. "So . . . you did . . . ma . . ." Her voice trailed off to a whisper for not Kitty, but Cayce Hamilton was leaning in negligent fashion against the door jamb, one hand thrust in the jacket of his dark suit.

"Hello, Shannon. May I come in?" His voice still bore the same deep timbre she remembered, reminding her of the luxurious feel of expensive velvet caressing her skin.

There were other things she remembered, too, things that were jumping out at her in her heightened awareness. Such as the dark thickness of his hair . . . the feel of it still fresh in her thoughts. The blue of his eyes, his gaze so compelling a person could feel the force, drawing them closer . . . closer, almost drowning in the bottomless pools. His nose still bore the mysterious hump, his lips more sensual than any man's had a right to be.

No, Shannon fleetingly thought, Cayce Hamilton hadn't changed in the slightest. If anything, he was more dangerous than ever.

Suddenly she became aware of staring, embarrassment bringing a flood of color to her face. "He . . . hello, Cayce. Please, come in." Shannon stepped aside, wishing she were anywhere in the world at the moment other than alone in her living room with Cayce.

Moments before his arrival the room had been a pleasant sanctuary, soothing and restful to Shannon. Now the space within the four walls seemed electrified by Cayce's disturbing presence, his unexpected appearance the catalyst capable of turning that electricity into a raging storm.

Shannon watched the progress of her guest as he walked on into the room, then paused, his gaze skirting the entire room before coming back to his hostess.

"Very nice, Shannon, very nice," he smiled. "This room reflects your warmth. It has much more personality than your last place."

"Really?" she answered coolly, remembering the long hours she'd put into decorating the apartment in St. Augustine. Of all the things she'd imagined them talking about when they did meet again, her decorating abilities certainly hadn't figured in the list.

Cayce's barely audible "Mmmmm" did little to soothe her discomfiture. "Since you're obviously not going out"—his eyes roamed over the green robe and the outline of her figure beneath—"why don't we have a cup of coffee and a nice cozy chat?"

"About what?" Shannon bluntly asked. This was certainly a switch from their last encounter. Having coffee and chatting like long lost friends simply wasn't Cayce's style. Besides, his sudden appearance was affecting her strangely. She'd spent months alternately missing and telling herself that she hated him. Seeing him in the flesh only served to remind her that Cayce Hamilton was dangerous—a man to be avoided at all cost.

Cayce merely smiled at her, less than pleased at her response to his suggestion. He turned and walked over to the sofa and sat down. "I can see that the old saying about absence making the heart grow fonder doesn't apply to you." He raised his arms and crossed his hands behind his head, his long legs stretched out before him. "Are you going to stand there all night with that disapproving frown on your face?" he innocently asked.

Shannon stifled the angry retort that sprang to her lips as she moved over to one of the wing chairs and sat down, favoring him instead with a cool smile. "It's refreshing to see that the last six months haven't changed your charming personality, Cayce. You're as thoughtful as ever."

"I do my best," he answered, deliberately misinterpreting her meaning.

"Why did you really come by?" she asked, tiring of the subtle insults that were being tossed back and forth. "I'd hardly consider our last meeting as being conducive to a lasting friendship, would you?"

The minute she saw the slow smile break the stern features of his face, Shannon realized she'd played right into his hands. "Ah, now I understand," Cayce drawled, plainly amused. "You're still miffed with me for not falling in with your childish game."

"I am not miffed!" she hotly declared. "I just think it's very presumptuous of you to appear suddenly on my doorstep and think we can become bosom buddies in less than five minutes. As you so *kindly* pointed out before, you and I can never be friends."

"Oh, dear," Cayce chuckled, not in the least perturbed by her acid tongue. "I can see that I really did get your back up. Will it help if I say I'm sorry?"

"Apology accepted," Shannon said softly. But she was still curious as to the reason behind his impromptu visit, and lost no time in restating her question.

"Let's suffice it to say that Kitty piqued my curiosity," he replied.

"About what?" Shannon asked suspiciously, glaring at him in a most unfriendly fashion.

"You. The amount of weight you've lost . . . the way you seem to be pushing yourself. Your entire physical condition."

"What condition, for heaven's sake?"

"When Kitty came back to the office all upset and going on about how hard you were pushing yourself, how tired you looked, I chalked it up to her usual manner of fussing over the people she loves. But when she wouldn't let the matter drop, I became curious to see for myself. She wasn't wrong. You look like a damn ghost of the woman I knew. Are you trying to kill yourself?" he harshly growled.

"Hardly," Shannon snapped. "As you well know, the law profession is a very demanding one. But even if what you say is true, I can't see what concern it is of yours. In case you've forgotten, I no longer work for you." How dare he barge in, checking up on her as though she were a child, not to mention his less than complimentary assessment of her appearance!

Forgotten was the headache, the sense of depression that had hovered over her earlier. The blood was now coursing through her veins at an amazing speed, each of her senses vitally alert. *Darn him,* she thought scowlingly, *I don't want his infuriating presence in my life. I'm not ready to cope.*

"The fact that you're no longer my secretary is a fact I'm well aware of, Shannon, each time I meet the steely-eyed gaze of the 'drill sergeant' Kitty found for me," he scowled. "I also knew that if I waited for you to get in touch with me, I'd be as old as Methuselah."

A mental picture of an aging Cayce, surrounded by a horde of fawning females, drew an involuntary quiver of her lips.

"I can see that you've gotten my drift," he said querulously.

At that point Shannon couldn't help but smile at the petulant sound of his voice, shaking her head at this incorrigible person before her. She knew her anger stemmed from an emotion far deeper than supposed dislike. In fact, her anger was as misleading as the façade of coolness she'd tried so hard to erect against Cayce.

Now, here he was, apologizing, a probable first in his entire life, and, in his own gruff way, concerned for her welfare. It was difficult to continue her private war against such actions.

Shannon also knew Cayce well enough to realize that if she continued to antagonize him, he would never leave. Any other man would have called and politely inquired after her health, perhaps even asked her to dinner. But not Cayce. He barged in with or without an excuse, not giving a tinker's damn whether or not it suited her.

"Would you care for coffee or a drink?" she asked, resigning herself to the fact that he would leave only when and if it pleased him, and not before.

"Why, how kind of you to offer, Shannon. Your generosity overwhelms me," he said mockingly.

CHAPTER FOUR

Rather than wait for Shannon in the living room as she fixed the coffee, Cayce propped his large body against the counter and watched her.

With an ease she was far from feeling, Shannon forced herself to remain cool and collected beneath the thorough scrutiny he was subjecting her to even as he questioned her about her work.

"They're a good, solid firm. Of course it may take longer to become a partner, considering that there's three ahead of you," he drawled innocently. "On the other hand, some lawyers prefer the quieter side of the profession. Research has its merits, but I'd find it terribly boring."

"I'm sure you would," she remarked heatedly, "and so do I. Unfortunately that's part of the price one must pay. But," she pointed out, "researching a case does have a way of making an inexperienced lawyer more cognizant of the law and the complexities therein."

"True," Cayce smoothly agreed, too smoothly to suit Shannon, who wondered what was coming next. "But wouldn't you really rather be learning the intricacies of defense by doing rather than by merely watching?" One dark brow arched as he waited for her reply. He seemed ready to pounce, however she answered.

Shannon took her time replacing the plastic lid on the can of coffee and then returned it to the cupboard. "Are you referring to your offer to practice with you?"

"Of course. It still stands. Anytime you're ready," he said accusingly. "Which just happens not to be anytime soon. You're still afraid of me, aren't you, Shannon?"

"Afraid? Of you? Certainly not," she hastened to add. "I simply preferred a change. Is that so difficult to understand?" She kept herself busy with arranging the cups on the tray . . . anything to keep from looking directly at him. "Everyone in the firm has been nice to me. That is, with the exception of Sam Jeffries."

"Oh? Does Jeffries feel threatened? I've met him on a number of occasions and he always seemed to have a chip on his shoulder."

"It's still there, believe me." Shannon grimaced.

"Would you like to wait in the living room till the coffee's ready?" she asked, becoming increasingly nervous by having to walk around him.

"Oh, no, it's almost dripped through," he said blandly, perfectly aware of her subtle attempt to get rid of him. "Let's get back to Jeffries. Perhaps I need to speak to him."

Shannon did look at him then with an expression akin to horror on her face. "Don't you dare!" she exclaimed. "That's all I need, you running about, smoothing the way for me. In nothing flat I'd be labeled as one of your . . . er . . ."

"Yes?" Cayce countered, the tiny network of lines at the corners of his blue eyes crinkling, his lips twitching suspiciously. "My what?"

Shannon chewed pensively at her bottom lip as she stared at him. "You know exactly what I mean, Cayce Hamilton, and I won't stand for it." She swung around and jerked open a drawer, removed two spoons and thumped them down on the tray.

"Why should it bother you if a few rumors do circulate? My name happens to carry a certain amount of clout, Shannon. And whether or not you approve, I will not stand by and let some bastard intimidate you just because he's not man enough to accept you as a professional equal."

Shannon's hands gripped the edge of the counter, her eyes tightly closed as she fought for control. *Dear heavens!* she wildly thought. *What can I say to get through to him? To allow my name to be linked with*

*his in any way other than strictly professional would
be suicidal as far as my reputation is concerned.*

She thought back to the tightrope of propriety
she'd been forced to walk during the eighteen
months she'd worked for Cayce. Never once had she
allowed herself to deviate from the cool, aloof role
she played. Well, almost never, she ruefully reminded herself. But even that one night in her apartment
hadn't been public knowledge. Knowing Cayce as
she did, and his propensity for disregarding society
and its rules, she'd be ruined in less time than she
cared to think about.

Shannon turned and glared at him, her eyes
stormy against the ridicule in his voice. "I made it
plain from the start that I wasn't interested in an
affair with you. I admired your legal expertise, and
I liked the nice salary you were offering. I think we're
even at this point. We both benefitted equally from
the arrangement," she stiffly informed him.

"Correction," he countered smoothly. "*You* benefitted, Shannon. I was used." Shannon felt the
humiliation steal over her face at his sharp criticism,
her eyes dropping. "You stood back from me as
though my touch would contaminate you. I found it
increasingly entertaining to goad you, trying to see
just how much you'd take before you told me to go
to hell. But you never did. Instead, you grew colder
and colder. Disapproval was stamped all over that
proud body in huge letters. It finally hit me during

78

that last six months that you possessed a number of the same traits as I do. Mainly determination."

"You make it sound like a disease," Shannon muttered, having gone quite pale under his attack. "At least I was honest with you."

"And you don't think I was? Honest with you, I mean." He pushed away from the counter and moved over to stand directly behind her. "Was I ever in any way deceitful with you, Shannon?" His breath fanned the soft tendrils of hair next to her ear. "Did I ever attempt to hide the fact that I wanted you? That I received considerable pleasure in looking at your slim body?" he murmured, his hands moving in featherlight strokes up her arms and across her shoulders to the coil of hair on her nape.

One by one, Cayce removed the pins that held it in place, letting them drop unheeded to the floor. When the last restrictive bits of metal were gone, the flaxen silk cascaded over Shannon's shoulders like a shimmering waterfall, completely covering Cayce's hands.

With a sinking feeling of standing on the crumbling edge of a precipice, Shannon held herself rigid beneath the warmth of his touch. There were two distinct forces within her, one urging her to surrender to the unspoken hold this man had over her, the other warning opposite in its meaning, forcing her to consider the folly of becoming involved with Cayce Hamilton. He was a rake, totally lacking in the sensitivity she admired in a man. However long it would have taken Shannon to come to a decision was never known. For at that moment, impatient with the sea of indecision surrounding her, Cayce took matters into his own capable hands.

With a firmness that brooked no argument, Shannon felt herself being turned completely around, the solid bulk of his chest replacing the attractive wallpaper at which she'd been staring.

"Look at me, Shannon," Cayce whispered gently, his hands beginning to awake the most gorgeous shivers of excitement along her spine.

"No," she whispered, groaning, her arms stiffly clamped to the sides of her slender body as she fought against the slowly stirring coil of desire in her stomach.

"Oh, honey," Cayce murmured crooningly. "Don't you know I can't resist such a challenge?"

Before Shannon could move, even think, she saw the already narrow space between them closing. She saw, then felt the unmistakable caress of his lips against the pearly-pink tip of her ear, then lower to the wildly beating pulse in her neck.

With a superhuman effort, she raised her hands and placed her palms against the wide wall of his chest, straining to loosen the hold on the back of her head, to stop the marauding fingers that were seeking and finding with unerring accuracy tiny points of arousal even she didn't know she had.

"Please, Cayce," Shannon cried out, her gray eyes glowing like deep, dark pools as they met the smold-

ering force of his blue eyes. "I'm not ready for this."
She turned her head in a half gesture of denial—of
indecision, the curtain of her hair clinging to the
dark sleeve of his jacket like a sprinkling of gold.

Heaving a deep sigh that in its very own raspy
sound bespoke regret, Cayce slowly shook his dark
head, an almost sad smile pulling at the corners of his
mouth as he stared down at her. "Why don't you ask
me to do something reasonable, like cutting off my
hand, hmmmm? It would be a far simpler thing to
do," he offered, his deep voice gruff with the gripping
emotion that enveloped them.

"I don't want you in my life," Shannon croaked as
Cayce removed one of her hands from his chest and
raised it to his lips, the tip of his tongue tracing an
erotic pattern against her palm. Instead of releasing
her hand, he threaded his long fingers between her
slender ones and rested their intertwined hands beneath his chin.

"Protest all you want to, honey, but I know differently, and so will you before we're through." Cayce
spoke even as his mouth swooped to take hers.

It was a matter of the expert and the unwilling
apprentice colliding in a battle where only one could
emerge the winner.

There was a tenderness in the kiss that surprised
Shannon. She'd been all set to resist further inroads
of assault upon her person. But for some strange
reason she was finding the incessant nibbling on her
lips by Cayce, the soothing caressing of his tongue,

to be very exciting. Added to that pleasure was the stroking motion of his large hand as it worked its way downward over her back, her small waist, and finally to the gentle swell of her buttocks.

Amid the considered efforts of tongue, lips, and hands, Shannon felt herself slipping further and further from reality, clinging closer and closer to Cayce's reassuring warmth. In her state of growing arousal, it became apparent that she wasn't content to be made love to. She found herself beset with an uncontrollable urge to touch Cayce, stroke the muscled firmness of his back, his shoulders. In fact, it was imperative that she do so.

Oh, God! she thought incoherently as the steady rise of desire crept with irrevocable certainty over her entire body. *I do believe I'll die from this exquisite feeling.*

When the first cooling breath of air whispered against the creamy softness of her pink-tipped breasts, and was just as quickly soothed away by an unbelievable warmth, Shannon gave a slight gasp of pleasure. With the warmth came a delicate circling of the turgid nipples that ended with a manipulation of the erect tips that had her shamelessly arching against that point of pleasure . . . thirsting . . . seeking . . . demanding a release to the raging inferno inside her.

Her mouth was now opened to Cayce's invading tongue, her own returning each thrust and parry with the boldness of a woman hungry for release from a submerged passion, one that had been too long denied.

Shannon was only barely aware of Cayce lifting her in his arms, of his determined-stride that took them to her bedroom and the beckoning softness of her bed.

Rather than rush what had grown into such inexplicable tenderness that he was visible shaken, Cayce let Shannon's slender form slide downward against the hard length of him.

Another time, another place, the change of scenery from the kitchen to the bedroom would surely have registered with Shannon. But the spell woven by Cayce was so complete it never occurred to her to resist. The desires of her body had taken over, blanking out the sane dictates of her mind.

In a trance of hypnotic fascination, she looked down at Cayce's hands as they pulled loose the ends of her satin sash. When the restricting band around her waist was released, the edges of the robe fell open to reveal the magnolia creaminess of her body. The thrust of her small breasts was proud, inviting. Her neat waist, slim hips, and long slender thighs beckoned Cayce to pay homage to their beauty.

"Ahh . . ." Cayce growled huskily, easing the emerald satin from her shoulders. "You're even more beautiful than I dreamed possible. There's nothing excessive about you, Shannon Bankston. You're just right, every single part of you, fashioned and fitted as though an expert craftsman had spent his life creating you."

Shannon wasn't embarrassed by the praise. The age-old feminine urge for woman to please man added a curious pride to her stature, to the bewitching hint of beguilment in her face as she raised her head and met the admiration in Cayce's gaze.

With a groan that became muffled in the fragrant thickness of her hair, he pulled her against his chest, his hands feverishly running over the fragile bones of her neck and shoulders, and lower, over the lithesome lines of her back, coming to rest on the slender swell of her hips.

"I've got to have you, Shannon," he rasped in a rough voice. "God! But you're in my blood. You have my permission to hate my guts in the morning, but here, and for now you'll be mine!"

In one clean swoop of his powerful body, Shannon felt the coolness of the rough-woven bedspread against her back. With a quickness that proclaimed more loudly than words his hunger for her, Cayce removed his clothes.

There was no shyness as Shannon watched the unveiling of his magnificent body. Often in the quietness of her mind she'd observed him—in court, striding about his office, even walking toward her, and had likened him to a large, predatory cat, the force within him barely leashed. The assessment remained, but added to it was his majestic bearing, the powerful strength emanating from him. He was perfection in form. He was man.

When he joined her, she instinctively opened her arms to receive him. When his mouth began a teasing exploration of her body, she unashamedly arched to meet it.

Slowly, excitingly, as though sampling each dish from a feast prepared for a king, Cayce let his lips close over first one, then the other rosy nipple, tugging at the sensitive points.

Shannon, her senses reeling under the masterful tutelage of such an expert, ran her palms over the breadth of his shoulders, reveling in the feel of his skin against hers, the pleasing male scent of him that filled her nostrils.

Her body was on fire. There was a restless movement of her limbs. One slim foot rubbed sensuously against the hair-rough skin of Cayce's leg as she silently pleaded for an end to the interminable torment he was subjecting her to.

In her mind's eye, the increasing punishment grew more intense. Mouth, hands, then tongue, gentle fingers, culminated in a shaft of desire that threatened her very sanity.

His large tanned hands caressed and squeezed her soft inner thighs, stroked the taut concave of her stomach, and ran possessively over her breasts. Her lips were tasted, the inner sweetness of her mouth sipped from time and time again before he finally ceased.

"I want to love you, Shannon," Cayce whispered against her ear. "I want to leave you wanting me more than anyone or anything in your life."

With her slim arms clinging to his broad, bronze back, Shannon was lost inside Cayce in a world that precluded all thoughts, all painful admissions that she'd been made love to before.

In the protection of his strong arms, Cayce carried her to levels of passion that rushed threateningly at her, then caressed her exposed vulnerability. Shannon lost count of the totally sweeping tides of emotion that held her on the knife-edged crests before the rush of shimmering velvet enclosed her body in its warmth.

The faraway sound of Cayce, crying out her name, the sudden paroxysm that shook him, signaled the beginning of the gentle descent from the world of exploding stars and brilliant firebursts.

It was sometime later, when the soft light of the moon had become obscured by a drifting cloud, that Shannon stirred. The unfamiliar pressure of an arm across her chest, a heavy leg thrown over her thighs, reminded her of the man beside her and the incredible events of the past few hours.

"You, Shannon Bankston, are a very silent lady when being made love to," that deep voice she knew so well softly teased her. "Do you know that your eyes become mirrors of your very soul? That a man could quite easily drown in their depths?"

Shannon accepted the gently spoken accolades

with a pensive silence. In her mind, that was now beginning to resume mastery over her thoughts, her emotions, she was surprised to see that she had endured the collision with Cayce, and had even survived the impact.

For over a year and a half she'd watched him as he'd gone through his "romantic" routine with each new girl friend. Three months was usually enough time for him to get to know, become bored with, and abruptly drop the unsuspecting victim.

From her vantage point as his private secretary, Shannon had seen the almost traditional red roses, most times accompanied by some expensive trinket, which was usually his way of ending each affair.

She had often wondered how it was possible for a person to be so disapproving of another, and yet secretly yearn to know, to experience an intimacy with that same individual.

She had tried to submerge her feelings by being openly mocking, clearly disdainful of Cayce. It was utterly stupid to entertain, even for a second, the idea that he was capable of a normal relationship.

Now she knew the unbelievable heights of ecstasy to which he could carry a woman—knew the warm, gentleness of his hands as they caressed her skin, drawing shudder after shudder of response. Shannon knew, without searching further, that she had been made love to by an expert.

But therein lies the problem, she sadly reflected. Cayce had perfected his technique in the act of seduction to as fine a point as his legal prowess. Both accomplishments were executed with only one thought in mind—that of overcoming his opponents, then skillfully delivering the *coup de grâce.*

"I've seen happier expressions on people in severe pain, Miss Bankston," Cayce growled, raising himself up on one elbow and resting his chin on his fist. There was a look of petulant discontent on his face, his blue eyes narrowing to mere slits as he watched the flicker of emotions that skipped across the delicate planes of her face. "I do hope you aren't going to try and convince me that you didn't enjoy our lovemaking, because I know differently."

Shannon, short of diving underneath the covers like an outraged virgin, had no choice but to meet the knowing intensity of his gaze. "Frankly that hadn't occurred to me. I'm sure you've been told the obvious often enough. However, in this instance, I don't think that's what you're angling for, is it, Cayce?"

"What the hell are you talking about?"

"I presented you with a challenge, didn't I? You've said so time and time again." Her voice became brittle and cold. "I'm not foolish enough to think you really care for me as a person . . . an individual. I've merely held out against you longer than any of the others. Well," Shannon briskly continued, swinging her legs over the side of the bed and rising to her feet, "consider my debt to you cancelled."

With deft movements of hands that belied the

quivering of her insides, she reached down for the emerald robe, slipped her arms into the sleeves, then tightly belted it around her waist. She looked down at Cayce, her enigmatical expression revealing nothing. "You say I used you for eighteen months. Well, now you have, I believe the correct word is—scored. We're even. I'd rather not see you again, Cayce. Other than professionally."

On remarkably steady legs Shannon walked to the bathroom and closed the door. She discarded the robe, turned on the shower, adjusted the temperature of the water, and stepped in.

Several minutes later, above the rush of the water, she heard the slamming of the front door.

CHAPTER FIVE

Life must go on. That's what Shannon kept repeating to herself in the days immediately following Cayce's visit to her apartment. Obviously the person responsible for such a sweeping, unromantic saying had been a man.

Men, Shannon thought as she momentarily forgot the case she was working on, the unqualified takers of the world. They made up the rules of life, played the game, and almost always emerged the winners. Especially a man such as Cayce.

But not this time, she silently promised herself for the umpteenth time, not this time. Cayce was a devious, unscrupulous swine. But, as he'd so delicately pointed out, she was in possession of a number of traits remarkably like the ones that made up his complex personality. It was those same traits Shannon was counting on to see her through the misery he'd created in her heart.

Although, she was forced to admit, his pointed absence since his startling visit had left her in a curious state of limbo. She'd been tempted several times to ask Kitty what was keeping her boss so busy, but always managed to nix the idea. Kitty was an incurable romantic. Already Shannon had caught the gleam of matchmaking in her roommate's eyes. Questions at this point would only bring about more complications.

Having firsthand knowledge of how underhanded Cayce could be, Shannon had been braced for a barrage of retaliative tactics. Not only had his wall of silence baffled her, it had also delivered a curious blow to her ego.

Hadn't he found her to be as attractive, as exciting as the other women he'd been involved with? Had he been disappointed in her as a lover? At least he could have called, she thought acidly, then immediately scolded herself. Wasn't this what she wanted? Hadn't she told him that any further relationship between them was impossible?

Not only did Shannon not entertain any ideas of an affair with Cayce, she mentally blanched at the thought of such a thing. He reminded her of one of the wild horses that roamed the western range. He was a free spirit. Loyalty to one woman would be totally alien to his nature.

On this particular late afternoon, as Shannon was gathering up what work she would take home with her, she was summoned to Josiah Hardwicke's office.

Without undue concern she stopped what she was doing and walked down the uncarpeted hallway to the gentleman's sanctuary. She was unable to control the rueful pull of her generous mouth as she became aware again, of the lack of grandeur gracing the offices of the founders of the firm. Obviously the three gentleman were of the old school and looked down their considerable noses at their younger colleagues, who rushed out and almost bankrupted themselves by hiring interior decorators and buying expensive furnishings. It was definitely a point to remember when she went out on her own.

Her discreet knock on one of the three front offices was answered by a gravelly voice bidding her to enter. There was a smile on her face as she met the direct gaze of Josiah, who had risen to his feet and was indicating that she should be seated.

"I apologize for detaining you, Miss Bankston, but I think you'll be pleased when you learn the reason," he informed her with his old-world courtesy, then lowered his tall, sparse frame back into his chair.

"It was no bother, sir, believe me," Shannon said in the same polite manner. It was the same way each of their conversations began. Mr. Hardwicke faintly apologetic, Shannon assuring him that he needn't be. It was simply an amusing exchange of courtesies that had created a soft spot in her heart for the supposedly crusty old man.

Josiah Hardwicke, the original founder of the firm, was still active in the practice of law, and very alert, in spite of his advanced age. Retirement was a word he refused to consider, and well he shouldn't; he could work rings around younger lawyers.

Shannon, by now used to the rather roundabout way by which he arrived at his reason for summoning her, sat back in the uncomfortable, straight-backed, leather chair and waited.

"Has Mr. Jeffries simmered down, or is he still carrying on like some wounded creature?" The question caught Shannon completely off guard.

"Er . . . I'm not sure I know what you're talking about, Mr. Hardwicke," she answered.

"Oh, come now, Miss Bankston. I've known Sam since the day he was born. He's the product of an overindulgent mother, which has considerably narrowed his opinion of a woman's place. I'm well aware of the unchivalrous manner in which he has been harassing you. However"—amusement twinkled in his blue eyes—"I've a pretty good idea you're more than capable of keeping the likes of Sam Jeffries in his place."

Shannon found herself embarrassed under the brief scrutiny. She honestly never assumed that any of the older men were aware of the friction between her and Sam. "I'm sure we'll be able to eventually arrive at some sort of truce."

"I doubt it, my dear, but I admire your professional behavior. Not to mention the fact that you've chosen to ignore a very noticeable thorn in your side." All the while he was speaking, his hands were busily shifting through the unbelievable clutter on his desk. Finally, coming upon the file he wanted, he favored Shannon with a devilish grin. "Let's see if we can't give you a little boost that will cause young Jeffries to be more concerned with worrying about his own career than spending time annoying you."

An hour later Shannon emerged from Josiah Hardwicke's office, armed with a bulging folder containing the particulars of *Gore vs. the State!*

Her head was still swirling with the unexpected windfall as she reentered her office. With the file clutched to her chest, she whirled around the room on feet that barely touched the floor. Her very first important case! Well, she mused with a shrug, not all hers. Mr. Hardwicke would be the attorney of record, but her name would appear as his assistant.

All during the drive home Shannon felt as though she were floating. Josiah Hardwicke had actually asked her to assist him!

Her exuberance was momentarily daunted when she burst into the apartment to find the living room empty. However, her disappointment was short-lived, her nose catching the delectable aroma coming from the kitchen, not to mention the softly flickering blaze in the fireplace.

"Kitty?" Shannon yelled. "I'm home."

Kitty's dark curly head appeared in the doorway, a comical expression on her attractive face. "So I see . . . and hear. What's up? You look ready to explode."

Shannon dumped her briefcase and shoulder bag on the sofa, then rushed toward the kitchen. "I have been asked by none other than Josiah Hardwicke to assist him in a rather important case!" she exclaimed, a huge smile splitting her face.

"Hey! That's terrific." Kitty laughed excitedly as she hugged her roommate. "If I hadn't already started dinner, we'd go out. Do you think you can tolerate as simple fare as manicotti?"

"Only if it's your mother's recipe," Shannon replied with feigned resignation.

"Hmmmm," Kitty murmured. "Remind me to go away when you try your first case. I'm not sure I can stand you."

"I know," Shannon replied unrepentently, filching a slice of cucumber from the large bowl of salad greens. "Aren't I terrible? I was also pleasantly surprised to learn that Mr. Hardwicke has been aware all along of Sam Jeffries and his cute remarks."

"Sounds like you've had quite a day."

"Oh, I have, I have."

"Why don't you freshen up while I get things ready? We can eat in about thirty minutes. By the way"—Kitty spoke over her shoulder as she prepared the garlic bread—"do you mind if we have a guest for dinner?"

"Not at all, Kitty, my love, not at all," Shannon sweepingly declared. "Tonight I could eat with the devil and never raise an eyebrow."

All during the time she was changing from the clothes she'd worn to work to a pair of yellow slacks and a cream-colored crocheted sweater, Shannon was still feeling the effects of her good fortune. She knew there would be hours of research and preparation before going to trial; after all, their client was accused of murder. But in spite of the hard work involved, she knew she'd been handed a veritable plum.

She was also quite certain that far from narrowing the breach between herself and Sam Jeffries, his jealousy over the case would merely intensify the ill feeling that existed between them.

It was while Shannon was removing the pins that confined her hair in its neat coil that she heard the doorbell. Kitty's guest, she told herself, and then began to brush her hair, deciding to leave it down for a change. The cool professional image she'd gone to such great lengths to create seemed out of place tonight, at variance with the bright-eyed, excited reflection staring at her in the mirror.

As she left her room she could hear the murmur of voices coming from the kitchen. She wondered who Kitty's friend was. Her roommate had several likely prospects on the string, but in the short while they'd been living together, Shannon had met only three. But knowing her friend as she did, and her unconscious habit of gravitating toward men with a marvelous sense of humor, Shannon was certain the evening would be enjoyable.

Just as she got to the door of the kitchen, Kitty, who happened to be reaching for the plates, turned and saw her roommate. "I was just about to come and get you. Our guests have arrived."

Shannon's answering smile was bright in response. She walked on into the room, then froze in her tracks, the smile becoming fixed. Not only was Don Heltz sitting at the table, but Cayce Hamilton as well, looking sexier than ever in dark trousers and a navy knit shirt.

Kitty, sensing Shannon's shock, broke the what could have been embarrassing moment by thrusting the dinner plates into Shannon's hands. "You set the table while I get the manicotti out of the oven."

She then put Don in charge of the wine, unobtrusively drawing him over to the counter, thrusting Shannon into the unpleasant position of standing next to Cayce, who, having risen to his feet when she entered the room, was leaning against the table in a relaxed manner, leaving Shannon with an almost uncontrollable desire to smash the plates over his detestable head.

"Kitty tells me that congratulations are in order, Shannon," Cayce drawled, warily eyeing the china she was holding in her hands. "Er . . . why don't you let me help you?" He reached over and took the plates and set them on the table. "Shall I get the knives and forks?"

"Please," Shannon murmured, suddenly finding it difficult to remain angry. Hadn't she known he would show up sometime? Besides, if she continued to stumble around like someone in a fog, Kitty would become even more suspicious.

The sight of Cayce, big as a mountain and just as unyielding, taking pains to place flatware and napkins in the precise position finally thawed the iciness of her features.

He happened to look up and catch Shannon as she attempted to smother her grin. "Would you care to share the joke, Shannon?" he taunted, albeit in a tone far removed from his usual one.

"No," she pertly countered. "But I am curious as to what brought you over for a visit." She closely watched the rugged features for some revealing fact. Had he assumed she would read more into their last visit, thereby using Kitty's presence as protection?

Cayce regarded her across the width of the table, his closed expression telling her exactly nothing. "Do you quiz all the men who call on you, Shannon? If there *has* to be a reason—and that's your opinion, not mine—then chalk it up to Kitty having mentioned that she was having manicotti for dinner. Look on me as . . . hungry." The ambiguity of his remark was not lost on Shannon.

She dropped her eyes against the gleam of amusement lurking in the depths of his blue gaze. "Then

I'm sure it will be worth your time. Kitty is a marvelous cook."

"Man does not live by bread alone, Shannon," Cayce said softly. "There are other things in this apartment that I find even more enjoyable than your roommate's culinary skills."

"Oh? I had assumed by your rather pointed silence that there was nothing here that could possibly interest a man with your taste." She wished she could have bitten off her tongue. She hadn't planned on his knowing that she'd been angered by his conspicuous absence, conspicuous in that it caused her to feel like a "one-night stand."

"As soon as we're alone, I'll see what I can do to change your mind."

You sap. You ninny, she wildly thought. *You would goad him. Why didn't you simply keep your mouth shut?*

"No fiery comeback, Shannon?" Cayce tensed underneath the laughing voices of Kitty and Don. "Have I for once managed to silence that wicked tongue of yours?"

Shannon looked up and met his gaze. "Only temporarily, counselor, only temporarily." The sparkle in her own gray orbs took the sting out of the words.

Dinner was a toss-up between a comedy of errors and a nightmare. Shannon found it almost impossible to function as a normal person with Cayce's overwhelming presence only a mere few inches to her right. In fact, each time she so much as wiggled a toe, she would find the hardness of his leg against hers, the brush of his arm against hers at his slightest movement. If she looked toward him, it was to find him watching her, his gaze seeming to bore into her very soul.

The only relief to the interminable meal came when Kitty proposed a toast to Shannon in honor of the new case. After all had touched glasses and sipped the wine, Cayce asked Shannon about it.

She briefly sketched in the details, unaware of the enthusiasm that warmed her voice. "Although, from looking at the facts we have now, it does present a challenge. The prosecution is in possession of a dying declaration."

"If you like, later I'll give you a couple of pointers to check on that might help you," Cayce offered. "Unfortunately I don't think Kitty or Don care for murder one as a topic of conversation at the dinner table," he grinned.

"How true!" Kitty emphatically declared. "I get all the law I can stand each day at the office. But you're in luck. We're going out, so you two ghouls can discuss the gory details to your hearts' content."

Shannon threw her friend a look that could only be described as deadly. She did not want to be alone with Cayce Hamilton. Not only could she not trust him, but where he was concerned she seemed to have no say in the traitorous response of her body.

Other than grabbing a jacket and going with Kitty and Don, uninvited, she had no choice but to sit calmly as they made their departure, smiling bravely as the sound of the door being closed echoed through the apartment.

"Well, Shannon. Now you're all alone with the big bad wolf," Cayce drawled silkily. "Are you going to bolt for your bedroom and lock the door, or are you going to try and retreat behind that frozen façade you've hidden behind for so long?"

"Why on earth would I do either?" she countered, sounding far braver than she actually felt.

"I see." Cayce shot her a strange look, his dark lashes shifting against the harsh angle of his cheek-bones. "Have you conveniently dismissed the time we spent together here in this apartment only a week ago?"

Shannon willed herself to remain calm, refusing to give in to the anger she was beginning to feel at his reference to what had taken place between them.

"I haven't recorded it in my diary as the most memorable event in my life, if that's what you're getting at. It was something we both enjoyed, but I doubt it will happen again."

"Oh? Have you now decided that sex is harmful or disruptive to you and your career?" he asked in mock innocence, his blue eyes holding a gleaming curiosity as they wandered over the silken fall of her hair, the firm thrust of her breasts against the softness of the sweater. When they eventually came back to her face, Cayce grinned at the frosty expression she wore, and chuckled. "If I were you, Shannon, I'd refrain from making bold predictions. You are as aware of me as I am of you. And contrary to that fertile imagination of yours, I'm not any more pleased by the realization than you."

For once Shannon was really speechless. She quickly looked away, uncomfortable beneath the visual examination to which he was subjecting her.

"I take it this is your night to wash dishes?" Cayce put the question to her in a brusque manner.

"Yes, yes, it is. Kitty does most of the cooking, so I do the cleaning up." She was somewhat daunted by his blunt confession. There were a number of questions buzzing in her head, but they would have to wait until later. She was forced to put aside her confusing thoughts when Cayce rose to his considerable height and began to gather up the dirty plates.

"You wash. I'll dry. Okay?"

"Yes, of course, that's fine," Shannon stammered, then silently cursed for allowing herself to be swayed by his glib tongue. Cayce Hamilton probably had more lines guaranteed to disarm a woman than hairs on a dog.

Rather than baiting her as was his usual habit, Cayce became the perfect guest. At first Shannon was wary of him, attempting to analyze each thing he said. But with skill and patience he soon had her laughing and talking naturally, and relaxed for the first time since the beginning of their stormy relationship. She stopped treating him with her usual suspicion and contempt.

By the time the dishes were taken care of, Shannon found, to her surprise, that she was actually enjoying a quiet evening with Cayce. *And that, my dear, is indeed something for your diary, if you kept one,* she reminded herself.

"Why the pensive expression?" he asked as he stood watching her fix a tray for their coffee. "Don't tell me we're about to become enemies again?"

Shannon smiled. "Actually I was thinking that this is the first time we've been together for any length of time without some sort of explosion," she confessed as she picked up the tray and headed for the living room.

"I think I resent you referring to the night we made love as an explosion. In my mind an explosion denotes a happening of fear that destroys, maims. We shared something infinitely beautiful and precious."

"Must you keep harping on that night?" Shannon asked in a dark voice. She placed the tray on the coffee table, then sank to the sofa and drew her feet beneath her.

"I must, Shannon," Cayce drawled as he dropped to the cushions beside her, "because you are trying so hard to bury it beneath the multitude of reasons you've concocted in your mind for not liking me."

An annoyed sigh passed through Shannon's lips as she digested this bit of bluntness. "Do you always refer to the more intimate moments you've spent with a woman each time you meet?" she asked in a biting tone. "I'd think even you would be gentleman enough to refrain from being deliberately embarrassing."

"Ahh, but that's where we differ, my love."

"I'm not your love," Shannon flared angrily.

"Yes, you are, Shannon. The problem is, you're too stubborn to admit it. As for what we . . . shared." He stressed the last word in a maddening fashion. "You're still equating sex such as you participated in with the less than admirable Jack Treen to our having *made love to each other*. There was and is no comparison, a fact I'll force you to accept if I have to rent a billboard in the heart of the city proclaiming such."

Shannon stared incredulously, her eyes round as saucers. "You're unbelievable!" she exclaimed, in her mind's eye visualizing such a thing happening without the slightest effort. She let her body relax, resting her head against the cushioned back of the sofa and stared at him. "Why are you doing this, Cayce? I mean, it's not as though we're strangers. We've traveled together, worked side by side for months." She grinned ruefully. "I became fairly used to your outrageous proposals, your attempts to shock me. Why have you chosen to pick it up again? You know I'm not ready for involvement of any kind."

"That, Shannon, is my secret. If I were to tell you, it's highly probable that you'd bolt like a scared rabbit." A smile of great gentleness touched his mouth, shaking Shannon to her very toes.

"May I ask you a question?"

"Shoot."

"Why do you persist in trying to shock me by your outrageous remarks?"

"I'm trying to shatter that controlled façade you keep slipping behind. Occasionally, only occasionally, you relax and become Shannon Bankston, a beautiful, sexy, gray-eyed witch. May I ask you a question?" he asked, a devilish twinkle in his eyes.

"Shoot."

"Will you have dinner with me tomorrow evening?"

"You know I'll be working late."

"So will I. Why not let me pick you up at your office around six? That's plenty late for you to be in that building by yourself," he frowned.

"Six o'clock it is."

"You see?" he smoothly countered. "You're learning not to argue so much. That's more than even I had hoped for."

His kiss, when she saw him to the door much later, was gentle but demanding. In a brief moment of fantasy Shannon thought to prove to herself that she could be in his arms and remain immune.

Cayce raised his head and smiled down at her. "Determined to the very end, Shannon?" he whispered, then took possession of her lips again.

This time there was no gentleness. Her moment of resistance had awakened a fire in him that soon had

Shannon clutching his broad shoulders as wave after wave of desire pulsed throughout her body.

Cayce's tongue and lips became a combined master of seduction, sipping and caressing the hidden mystery of her mouth. His hands moved with languid ease over her body, possessive and sure in their touch.

With no overt deliberateness on her part, but rather an insatiable need that was clawing at her, Shannon found herself responding to Cayce, and then in the whirlwind of her passion there was a subtle changing of the roles as she became the seducer.

Her hands, that had only moments before sought the reassuring firmness of his broad shoulders, now caressed that same inviting width of muscle and firm skin with sensitive fingertips that were on fire with wanting to consume.

Her lips, that had obediently responded, were now hungrily seeking in their quest to transmit and at the same time draw Cayce into the shimmering, excruciatingly beautiful urgency that was surrounding her.

Uncannily perceptive of her needs, and himself caught in the same web of intuitive awareness that had always existed between them, Cayce met Shannon's surprising capitulation with a muttered groan of satisfaction.

With an exquisite, almost painful dalliance that shielded his raging desire, Cayce eased his large palms over the rigid tautness of her back, briefly pausing to softly clasp the smooth slimness of her waist, then on downward to press her hips against his thighs.

He raised his head and stared into her eyes, their swirling gray depths intriguing him with the open invitation he saw there, and at the same time there was uncertainty, a ghost of a hint of fear.

"Moments ago you were telling me how you weren't ready for personal involvment with me," he murmured, his voice soft and husky. "Now your body is crying out for tenderness, for love in a language that only a stone could ignore. Which one do I listen to, princess? The quiet, dignified Shannon Bankston, attorney? Or do I go with my gut feeling, that that same young woman refuses to accept the inevitable?"

Shannon returned his gaze, unable to break the compelling link between them. "I don't know," she whispered in a tortured voice. "But I do know that at this moment I want you."

A shudder so brief that only the extreme closeness of their bodies made Shannon aware of it coursed Cayce's body. He brought one hand up and clasped the back of her head, easing her face to rest against his chest. "I know, sweetheart, I know," he gruffly rasped, then swung her off her feet and laid her before the fireplace.

With a tenderness that brought a shimmering mist to her eyes, Shannon let her clothes be removed—something deep within her at that particular moment whispering that this huge, intimidating man would never deliberately hurt her.

Before Cayce could tug the tail of the navy knit shirt from the waistband of his trousers, Shannon found herself pulling at the material. Once it was free, she ran her hands beneath the soft shirt, touching and feeling the warmth and strength of his broad back and shoulders.

Becoming impatient with her maddening touch that was causing him to fast approach the breaking point, Cayce caught Shannon by the shoulders and eased her back from him, then finished the task of undressing himself with quick, deft movements.

"I can only take so much, you little witch," he growled, his eyes staring hungrily at the delicate loveliness of her body. The dimness of the single lamp and the flickering softness of the glowing coals in the fireplace cast a sprinkling of gleaming highlights in the thick beauty of her hair that nestled temptingly on her shoulders.

Without ever breaking the unbelievable spell that was being woven between them, Cayce reached for a pillow from the sofa and gently placed it under Shannon's head. He then reached for Shannon's hand and drew it along his broad chest, delighting in her soft touch.

This time, unlike before, there was no denial in Shannon's body as she moved against the pleasure being awakened by the continuous motion of Cayce's hands over her body.

The creamy softness of one breast glowed brightly against his hand as he held the fragile weight in his cupped palm. When he leaned down and took the painfully quickened tip between his lips, Shannon gasped.

Her hands that had been moving over his chest suddenly clasped his dark head and pressed him closer, shamelessly inviting his touch. She moved her hips sensuously beneath Cayce's, inwardly longing for the ultimate moment, the total surrendering of her womanliness into his hands that would bring the release she was aching for.

"Am I making love to Shannon Bankston, attorney, or Shannon, the bewitching enchantress?" Cayce murmured as his arms cradled her to him and he let the weight of his body press against hers, blending their bodies into one.

"Does it really matter?" Shannon whispered against the exquisite warmth pervading her mind, her senses.

"Oh, it will, my darling, it will," Cayce said in a softly muffled voice, his face buried in her hair, "and sooner than you think."

CHAPTER SIX

Having awakened the next morning at the unholy hour of six o'clock, Shannon struggled against full wakefulness. But after several minutes of tossing and turning, she decided it was useless to put off the inevitable and got up. She turned off the alarm, then padded to the bathroom.

After splashing several handfuls of cold water on her face, she ventured a cautious peek into the mirror from between spread fingers, surprised and then thankful to see that her eyes looked normal enough in spite of the sand she was sure had been dumped beneath each of her lids during the night.

As she went through the morning ritual of brushing her teeth and removing the snarls from her hair,

Shannon reflected on the reason for her nocturnal unrest—Cayce Hamilton.

Last night had been everything she'd ever dreamed it would be. *Dreamed it would be,* she thought scornfully, and then stared soberly at her reflection in the mirror. *Oh, yes, my dear. You most definitely have spent countless moments dreaming of Cayce making love to you. He's been in your blood since that first moment you walked into his office. Last night was merely the first time you allowed yourself to give in to your true feelings. Now what?*

"Now nothing!" Shannon muttered in disgust as she turned from the revealing face in the mirror. For regardless of how she privately thought—and at this stage of her life she was totally confused—Cayce was tricky. That was part of his strategy, his plan of seduction, she reminded herself. If submission wasn't gained by the considerable force of his charm, he would easily switch his campaign to one of gentle persuasion, gaining his victim's confidence and then striking with no hint of warning.

Trouble is, she told herself as she left the bathroom and headed for the kitchen, *I've missed the unscrupulous devil, and he knows it. Add to that the fact that I came on to him like some love-starved adolescent and you have the classic case of Cayce Hamilton playing the tune and me dancing to the music!*

She was reminded of his touch on her face the night before as he was leaving, the fingers of one hand softly tracing the rosiness of her cheek. "The next time you decide to seduce me, Shannon, you'd better make sure your roommate is away for the night. Making love to you and then leaving you is not my style."

While she was putting on the coffee, pouring the orange juice, and readying the bacon to be broiled, she found herself in a quandary as to what to do. She'd been burned too badly by Jack ever to indulge in a frivolous affair with anyone, especially Cayce. Perhaps she was an oddity, but she was also one of those unfortunates who gave her all to a relationship. She'd learned that much from her first adolescent fling.

She'd thought—naively so—that Jack's love was as steady and enduring as a mountain. Unfortunately her mountain's strength proved to be about as dependable as the land undermined by the San Andreas fault!

To say the disappointment, the embarrassment she'd suffered at Jack's hands had left untold scars would be leaning toward the dramatic. He had caused Shannon pain. But out of that pain had grown a single-minded resolve that never again would she allow herself to be used by a man in such a manner.

While all the other men of her acquaintance since Jack had been kept at a friendly distance, she'd found herself unable to deal with Cayce. She vacillated from hot to cold where he was concerned, damning him for his deplorable role as a rake and at the same time secretly wondering what he would be like as a lover.

Well, now she knew! But instead of leaving her soothed and comforted, Shannon was uptight. She knew she was no match for him when it came to the subtleties of the game, her inexperience causing an enormous void between them. Her only recourse, she reasoned, was to look upon him as some contagious disease that only time and determined effort would eradicate.

She was on her second cup of coffee, a frown creasing the smoothness of her forehead, when Kitty entered the kitchen. Shannon regarded the mussed hair of her roommate, the tautness of her features and grinned.

"A fun evening?" Just the barest hint of sarcasm edging her voice.

"Fantastic," Kitty groaned, blindly reaching into the cupboard for a mug and filling it with coffee. She carried her drink over to the table and sat down very carefully, one hand cradling her head. "I think it was close to three A.M. when I got home." She shuddered.

"You are the only person I've every known who judges an evening's success by the degree of exhaustion you feel the morning afterward."

"Do I detect the soft hissing of our feline counterpart in your tone?" Kitty asked as she took a sip of the hot coffee. "Did you and Cayce have words?"

"Off and on," Shannon admitted, shrugging. "Although I must admit he was more pleasant, more human than I've ever known him to be. I am curious, though, why you didn't tell me he would be joining us for dinner?"

"Quite simple. He asked me not to."

"Do you always do everything he asks?" Shannon asked pointedly.

"Okay, I'm sorry. I made a mistake. But for a supposedly bright girl, you're incredibly dense about some things, namely Cayce Hamilton," Kitty sharply retorted. "Regardless of your opinion of him, he is interested in you. He asked a simple favor of me and I obliged him. Was it really so bad?"

"No, not bad. It was a surprise, that's all. I'm not ready for any sort of involvment, Kitty, and Cayce knows it. I want to practice law without any sort of emotional entanglements nagging at me."

"Is it necessary to live in a cloister to accomplish your goal in life?" Kitty asked in her most common-sense approach. "You've pushed yourself terribly to get through school. Now you have a nice position with an excellent firm." She spread her hands, palms up. "What's wrong with a little socializing?"

"With Cayce?" Shannon asked.

"You act as though he's some sort of pariah. He's well-respected in his field—very popular in his circle of friends. His reputation where the ladies are concerned is part truth, part conjecture. And anyway, you'll have to admit that women aren't exactly shy about pursuing him."

"Nor he in welcoming them," Shannon snapped.

"You're incorrigible," Kitty sighed. "Why shouldn't he enjoy life? He's single, rich, and sexy as hell. Honestly, sweetie, you've lost all perspective where your former boss is concerned."

"Oh?" Shannon asked archly. "Well, to prove to you that I'm not being unduly critical of your favorite playboy, I am having dinner with him this evening."

"Really? Did he hold a gun to your head?"

"A moment of weakness is more like it. I'll probably regret it before the evening is over," she ruefully remarked as she got up and began preparing breakfast.

"Don't be so fainthearted, Shannon. Cayce may have his faults, but he would never do anything to hurt you," Kitty said.

Later, as she drove her vintage VW to work, Shannon wondered at Kitty's faith in Cayce. She knew Kitty had worked for him for a number of years. And yet she still had nothing but nice things to say about her employer. Kitty wasn't some starry-eyed individual. She was one of the most level-headed women Shannon knew, her opinions giving Shannon a great deal to think about.

Once she arrived at the office, all thoughts of Cayce, good or bad, were placed on hold. Mr. Hardwicke wanted to see her regarding the Gore case. Another case she'd been working on was due to go to court in a few days, necessitating a conference with one of the other junior partners, who was the attorney of record.

Josiah smiled at Shannon as she joined him in the library, its walls banked from floor to ceiling on all sides with endless tomes of legal doctrine. "I'm sure you're beginning to think you'll never get out of this room, my dear."

She chuckled at his correct assessment of her thoughts. "It has occurred to me that a cot would be a nice addition to the furnishings."

"Perhaps the Gore case will enable you to see another side of the law, where the fruits of many hours of preparation become the means by which you either win or lose the battle."

"I must admit I'm excited. Even though I was associated with two excellent lawyers while I was in school, this is different," she confessed.

"That's understandable. I do hope you realize how fortunate you were in working with Cayce Hamilton and Cyrus Whittaker. They're both a credit to the profession. I was pleased to learn that Cayce has finally decided to move closer."

"Have you known him very long, Mr. Hardwicke?" Shannon asked, strangely curious for the older man to voice an opinion.

"Oh, yes. His grandfather took a chance on me when I was fresh out of school and struggling. He retained me to represent his brokerage firm." He smiled, his blue eyes bright. "I can truthfully say,

116

Miss Bankston, that it still stands out as one of the highlights of my career."

"In spite of the cases you've defended and won?"

"Yes," he answered unequivocally. "I worked my way through law school much the same as you did. When I got my degree, I didn't have two pennies to rub together. But in those days it was possible to borrow on your expectations. People trusted one another, believed in helping each other.

"I'd been practicing for about six months and was beginning to wonder if starvation wouldn't get me before the fame and fortune I'd envisioned during those years of study, when Archibald Hamilton paid me a visit. He was flaming mad and had fired the prestigious firm out of Atlanta. At the conclusion of a twenty-minute conversation I was hired." He chuckled at the look of incredulity on Shannon's face. "A scant twenty minutes. Archie Hamilton wasn't a man to waste time. I often told him, after we became friends, that he was wasted in the world of stocks and bonds. He would have been a fine lawyer."

"I'm surprised you didn't offer his grandson a position with your firm," Shannon said thoughtfully.

"I did," Josiah nodded. "But to Cayce's way of thinking that would have been trading on his grandfather's name. He's as daring and determined as Archie. Though a generation separated them, they're remarkably alike."

There was a poignant silence as Shannon patiently

waited for the old man's memories to return to the treasure trove of his mind. Memories played an important role in the lives of the aged, and Josiah Hardwicke, for all his wealth, was no exception.

"Now," he announced after the brief silence, "let's get down to the business of hand, mainly that of saving James Gore's neck."

Any doubts Shannon might have had regarding the sharpness of the older man's mind were put to rest as the conference progressed. For the first time since leaving Cayce, she was privileged to watch an expert at work. Though their styles were different, Josiah reached his goal in other ways. He was wily as a fox, unashamedly using his age as a weapon of disarmament. Oh, yes, Shannon thought with a smothered grin of appreciation, it would be a pleasure to watch Mr. Hardwicke at work.

During the middle of the afternoon, Shannon closeted herself in her office with the Gore file and began studying each scrap of paper. So far her mental picture of the man and his crime was merely a reflection of Josiah's thinking. In order to help prepare the case, she knew it was imperative that she form her own ideas, her own impressions.

James Gore was accused of shooting Mr. A. Cronin. Mr. Cronin died approximately one hour later. Both men, it was later learned, had been seeing Valerie Drury, a wealthy married woman. The crime took place at the home of Mrs. Drury, supposedly while the "lady" was out of the room.

The accused vehemently denied the charges against him, with his "lady friend" equally vocal in her accusations. Her statement to the police, that upon hearing the shot she rushed to the living room and found Cronin lying on the floor, shot in his right shoulder, and that he'd named Gore as his assailant, weighed heavily for the prosecution. Their case was mainly founded on the theory that Gore committed the crime, then panicked and ran. The gun, a small caliber, hadn't been found.

It was well after five o'clock, and Shannon could hear the sounds of the others leaving, when suddenly there was a knock on her office door. Before she could call out, the door opened.

"Hello, Sam. What can I do for you?" she asked in a resigned voice as Sam Jeffries strolled in and sat on one corner of her desk.

There was a sullen frown on his face as he let his gaze touch on the opened file, its contents scattered over the desk. "I hear old Hardwicke asked you to assist him on the Gore case. There'll be quite a bit of publicity from that one."

"I'm sure there will be," Shannon reluctantly agreed. She wasn't at all anxious to discuss the case with Sam. He was conniving and sneaky. She wouldn't put it past him to try and discredit her in some way.

"How did you do it, Shannon?" he asked, a sneering grin on his face. "Josiah is rather old for you, isn't he?"

Instead of reacting in what she imagined Sam would consider a purely feminine way, by slapping his detestable face, Shannon calmly gathered the pages of the file together and stacked them in a neat pile. She rose to her feet, placing her fists on the desk and leaned forward. "Get out of my office, Sam," she demanded, her voice very quiet, very firm.

"Come now, Shannon," he said with the same degrading inference. "The whole firm is buzzing with how you capitalized on an old man's vulnerability—not to mention Cayce Hamilton's considerable influence."

"One more word, Jeffries, and I promise you, you will be wearing false teeth," came a deep voice from the opened doorway, the lurking menace in the deadly tones sending a scattering of goose pimples over Shannon's arms.

She looked beyond Sam and saw Cayce's towering build framed in the aperture, his face dark with rage.

Her uninvited guest shot from his perch on her desk as though jet propelled, which was a mistake, because he was left standing in the middle of the room, looking for all the world like a small, scared boy, who had been caught misbehaving.

"Er . . . hello, Cayce," he stammered, a profusion of red creeping upward from his scrawny neck and slowly stealing over his features.

"Mr. Hamilton to you, Jeffries. Only my friends call me Cayce, and you definitely do not qualify." Cayce delivered his words stingingly. He came on-into the room, not breaking stride till he reached Shannon's side. Before she could guess his intentions, she felt the firm warmth of his arm slide around her waist, his palm covering the pivotal point of her hip.

"How are you, honey?" he huskily murmured, then bent down and brushed her forehead with his lips. He raised his head, his gaze boring contemptuously into Sam Jeffries's frightened face. "Was there something else you wanted with Miss Bankston, Jeffries?"

"No, no, nothing else," the younger man hastily said.

"Good. Then I suggest you get the hell out of here. Oh, by the way, Jeffries. If I hear, if I even suspect that you're harassing my fiancée again, I'll come after you. Understood?"

The full meaning of what he'd done and the impending punishment if he didn't make tracks hit Sam at the same time. His outright panic at the thought of Cayce Hamilton throttling him gave added impetus to his flight from the room, his muffled "Understood" floating over his shoulder.

Shannon remained in her near paralyzed state of shock for several seconds, her colleague's cruel insinuations overshadowed by Cayce's casually addressing her as his fiancée.

Shock gave way to anger as the full impact of what he'd done rushed over her. Knowing Sam Jeffries as she did, and his annoying habit of spreading gossip, the entire firm, as well as half the people in town would hear the news by morning.

"Mr. Hamilton," she said firmly as she bowed her head in an attempt to cope, her fists still bracing her upper body, "will you please explain why you were stupid enough to say what you did in front of Sam Jeffries?" She turned her head and looked up at him. "What on earth possessed you to make such a statement?"

Cayce returned her angry glare with his own level gaze, not in the least bothered by her outburst. "I may be seven kinds of a bastard as far as you're concerned, Shannon, but I've never tried to blackmail a woman, or a man, for that matter, the way Jeffries was fixing to do you."

"Blackmail?"

"Yes. If my temper hadn't gotten the best of me, you'd have heard that slime suggest rather strongly that you withdraw from the case or risk having your reputation smeared."

"I would never have let it get that far. I'm sure he was only bluffing," Shannon feebly protested. It suddenly dawned on her that Cayce's arm was still draped around her waist; one whole side of her was pressed against his much taller frame. She moved away from him, ignoring the lingering way his fingers trailed ever so lightly across the lower part of her spine in the process.

"Were you ready to call his bluff, Shannon?" Cayce sharply asked, clearly annoyed with her.

"Were you ready to have your name bandied about as my latest mistress? Perhaps even the last fling for the aging Josiah Hardwicke?"

"Those are vile accusations, and you know it," Shannon muttered, her present mood of unhappiness sending her over to the window. She hugged her upper body with both arms, still shaken, angered by the sudden turn of events. Damn Cayce and Sam! They had no right to ruin what had been a beautiful day.

There was a perceptible hardening of Cayce's features as he watched her, the dejected slump of her shoulders boding ill for Sam Jeffries. "The accusations are vile, honey, I'm not denying that. It's also unfortunate that with all the decent lawyers around, you have to come in contact with one of the few undesirable bastards in our midst. I frightened the living hell out of him, but he can still do you harm."

Shannon turned and stared at him over her shoulder. "Is the case really that important to him?"

"Hell, yes, it's important," Cayce growled. "But Josiah chose you, and that's what infuriated Jeffries. He's got better than a year's experience on you, and was determined to get the case any way he could."

"It sounds so vicious."

"It is, honey. You'll always find some son of a bitch ready to try and do you in, damning you for daring to intrude on what they consider their turf, living in fear of having their manly rights wrenched from them by a woman."

"You tried to warn me, didn't you?" she huskily asked. "You could see what was ahead for me."

Cayce took one step toward her, then stopped. Instead, he turned her chair around and sat down, his long legs stretched out, his arms raised, hands clasped behind his head.

"Is that defeat I'm hearing in your voice, Shannon? Are you ready to throw in the towel at the first hint of unpleasantness?" he drawled lazily, his blue gaze mocking.

Shannon turned from the window and stared defiantly at him. "The first hint of trouble, Mr. Hamilton? Just what would you know about the trouble I've been having? My *trouble* with Sam Jeffries started the day I walked into this office, and it's steadily grown," she lashed out, venting all the frustrations, the anger she'd been keeping inside her for months.

How dare he sit there like some all-knowing, all-seeing seer, dismissing the strain she'd been under as some sort of copout! How dare he!

"Get the hell out of here, Cayce Hamilton, and take your unwanted observations with you!"

There was an added brilliance to her gray eyes as they impaled Cayce. Her stance, the added color in her cheeks attested to the unleashed fury raging inside her.

"Did you hear me?" she stormed in a manner totally out of character for Shannon. "I'm sick of you and your damn meddling in my life, sick of Sam

Jeffries . . . of all men. In fact, *I hate men!*" Her voice began to wobble uncertainly as her tirade slowed. "N-now, not only do I have one idiot after my job, I have you announcing that I'm your fiancée." The tears that had been threatening slowly spilled over and stole down her face. She felt cornered, and she was vulnerable.

Shannon watched through a blur as Cayce uncoiled from his lounging position in her chair and rose to his feet. She saw him moving toward her with determined ease. "Don't you dare touch me," she cried, stumbling backward in her attempt to evade his touch. "Don't touch me!" But even while she was crying out against this further invasion, she felt the iron grip of Cayce's fingers on her shoulders, the gentle but firm pressure of his arms as they folded her against the solid bulk of his chest.

"Get it out, honey, get it all out," he whispered, one large hand stroking her hair, its touch playing havoc with the neatness of the flaxen silkiness.

The quiet rumbling of his voice and the gentle soothing of his hands amassed the conflicting emotions within her into one teary eruption as she gave way to the sobs she'd been holding back.

Shannon's momentary deviation from her role of the cool professional left her feeling unclothed, the only comfort coming from the chest beneath her cheek, the steady rhythm of Cayce's heart.

Once started, the flow of tears rushed forth in torrents. It seemed to Shannon that she was crying for each day of the last five years of her life, for each battle she'd fought in order to gain a toehold in the male-dominated profession she'd chosen, and the last few months as she'd struggled to maintain that hold.

In the midst of the tearful outpourings of her heart, she found herself clinging to Cayce, drawing strength from him, knowing instinctively that he would sustain her.

As the tide of emotion began to ebb, it occurred to Shannon that there was very little embarrassment at having Cayce see her in such a state. Perhaps it came from knowing him as she did, the manner in which he lived his life. Or it could have been that Cayce Hamilton, ably discerning in each individual that tiny chink in their armor, accepted her tears, her outburst as a natural healing process. He simply held her, never condemning with words or action.

In the midst of the last sniveling moments, Shannon felt a large, soft square of cloth being thrust in her hand, with a gruff order to "Mop up."

She did as she was instructed, knowing that her usual sharp comeback in answer to one of his commands would be completely out of line. Further reflection revealed that there was something infinitely amusing and, at the same time, disconcerting to be held and comforted by a rake! Especially one who had made love to her. A man unsure of his masculinity might have taken advantage of a woman in tears. But not Cayce. And at that moment it hit Shannon like a bolt of lightning; there was considerable difference in Cayce the playboy, and Cayce the man.

The discovery left her curiously aware and more than a little wary of the huge man supporting her, of the deep feelings she was trying so hard to ignore. Unfortunately the dictates of one's heart cared nothing for a career, the impatient years spent in achieving that career. The heart was an entity unto itself, and Shannon knew she was going to have to deal with her heart's desire in the very near future.

CHAPTER SEVEN

Shannon stepped back from the close circle of Cayce's arms, her eyes lowered to her fingers that were attempting to fold his handkerchief. It seemed that through the simple task of returning the white square to its original pristine neatness would blot out the next few minutes.

"Are you all right?" Cayce asked in the gravelly fashion she was accustomed to, his hands sliding down her arms to gently clasp her wrists.

"Yes," she nodded, still refusing to look up. "I'm fine now."

"Then look at me, Shannon." He removed the handkerchief from her nervous fingers and returned it to his inside jacket pocket.

"You're a bully," she quietly remarked, a ghost of

a smile teasing her lips as she met the striking force of his bright blue gaze. "You're also a very disruptive influence in my life, Cayce Hamilton."

Something very close to a sigh escaped him, the sound so slight it went unnoticed by Shannon. "A crime to which I'll gladly admit my guilt." There was a guarded alertness about him, as if he held something precious within his grasp and was fearful of its being damaged in some way.

"I'm not ready, Cayce," she whispered into a quietness that had suddenly turned from a hysterical outburst to a moment not unlike others she'd been caught up in with this man.

No matter how long it was between the confrontations, the results were always the same, leaving Shannon with a sense of impending uncertainty. From the first moment she'd walked into his office, her pride bruised, her dreams shattered, she'd recognized Cayce as a potential enemy—an enemy she'd tried to ignore.

"Stop looking so damned scared," he snapped, his voice cutting into the eerie silence. "One would think I'd threatened your life, when all I've done is come to take you to dinner."

"You're early," Shannon reminded him for lack of something better to say.

"Don't quibble, Shannon." He gave her a flicker of annoyance through narrowed lids. "Why don't you go fix your face while I make a couple of phone calls?"

129

"Of course. After all, it would really set the tongues wagging for Cayce Hamilton's fiancée to appear in public with her face all blotched and red from crying, wouldn't it?" She was peeved at being reminded of her moment of weakness.

"Would you care to risk it?" he asked in a deceptively bland voice. "If you can stand the speculation, I'm sure I'll have no trouble enduring the same."

"No, thanks," Shannon snapped. She walked around to the desk and reached into the drawer for her purse. "Anytime I'm out with you, I like the event to be as inconspicuous as possible."

Sometime later Shannon was walking beside Cayce, his palm cupping her elbow as they made their way to a cozy table near a large window in one of the nicer restuarants in Jacksonville. After being seated, and during Cayce's low-voiced conversation with the waiter on the choice of drinks, Shannon let her gaze scan the room in an attempt to get a firm hold on herself.

Her offhand remark to Kitty at breakfast, of how having dinner with Cayce would probably be a regrettable experience, had thus far been correct. Although, in all fairness, his timely intervention during her conversation with Sam Jeffries was appreciated, the blunt way in which he cut short Sam's nasty insinuations but certainly not his own casual reference to her as his fiancée. That little matter still remained to be settled, which it would be before the evening was over.

Of their own accord, her eyes lost interest in the other people in the restaurant and returned to Cayce. He looked as though he'd just stepped from his apartment, rather than having worked all day. He looked freshly showered, the superb cut of his faultlessly tailored suit emphasizing the undeniable fitness of his build. The sharp contrast of the white shirt against the tanned features of his neck and face bespoke a man who stayed out of doors a great deal of the time.

Shannon also knew there were callouses on his palms from the work he did when relaxing on his ranch. That much of his mistaken image she grudgingly gave him. She'd never seen his ranch, located in the vicinity of Kissimmee, but she'd heard conversations with his foreman and had seen enough of the correspondence while working for him to know that it wasn't merely a toy.

All in all, she was finding it increasingly difficult to keep Cayce confined to the boxed-in image of the irresponsible playboy, when not on a case, in which she'd so easily relegated him.

It had served her purpose to think of him that way, as well as providing her with an invaluable weapon against his captivating personality. Now she wasn't finding it so easy. Cayce wasn't cooperating and it irritated her. She didn't want to be forced to see the nicer side of him—his profligate image was less complicated to deal with.

Besides, she reminded herself, she'd seen the

women come and go in his life. She'd seen the hurt mirrored in their faces when Cayce would end the affair. Whatever good there was in him, and Shannon was forced to admit that he possessed a few redeeming qualities, was far overshadowed by the flagrant disregard with which he used members of her sex.

She also knew that juggling a career and a close relationship with Cayce was more than she could handle. She certainly wasn't about to throw away the last five years of her life for a few months of becoming Cayce Hamilton's woman.

"What little trick are you planning now, Miss Bankston?" Cayce asked, breaking into the reflective state into which she'd drifted. "Since I'm usually the object of your less than pleasant thoughts, I'd like to know what's bothering you this time."

"That ridiculous remark you made to Sam Jeffries, referring to me as your fiancée," she replied. "That really wasn't necessary, Cayce."

"I thought so, Shannon, and I'm not the least bit sorry." He grinned. "Does that shock you?"

"No," she snapped. "It merely confirms my earlier opinion. However, there's no point in worrying about it now. What concerns me is how to stop the rumors from spreading."

"Why bother? If it's thought that you're my fiancée, you won't be bothered by every Tom, Dick, and Harry wanting to go out with you. You can devote all your time to the practice of law." He met her narrowed gaze as innocently as a babe. "That is what you want, isn't it?"

"Of course it is! But I've never intended that my social life be completely cut off, and you know it."

Shannon sat back in her chair and regarded Cayce with a malevolent stare. "I don't want to be paired with just one man, Cayce, and that includes you."

"Shannon . . . Shannon." He shook his head as he studied her, an expression of profound resignation softening the harshness of his roughhewn features. "Don't you think it's time we stopped this little charade we've been playing at for so long?"

"I've no idea what you're talking about." She knew exactly to what he was alluding, but she would never give him the satisfaction of admitting it.

"Then let me put it into simpler words, Shannon," Cayce drawled. "I've wanted you since you waltzed into my office nearly three years ago. I respected your outlandish notions of propriety as long as you were in my employ. But that's changed now. You're no longer my secretary, and I'm growing damn weary of this cat-and-mouse game."

"Indeed!" Shannon sarcastically exclaimed, her pulses thudding. "Don't I have a say in the matter?" A faint flush swept over her cheeks.

"No."

A further exchange was halted by the waiter with their drinks. Shannon lifted the drink to her lips, watching Cayce over the rim as she sipped the smooth mixture.

"Is that why you chose Sam as the first to know of our . . . er . . . hypothetical engagement?"

"How astute," Cayce said. "I prefer to have an uncluttered field when I'm interested in a woman."

Shannon set her drink on the table with a thud and leaned forward, her gray eyes flaring with the warning signs of battle. "Has anyone ever told you that you are a conceited bastard?" Her voice was so soft Cayce was barely able to hear her.

A slow grin broke the curve of his lips. "Now that you mention it, yes. For far longer than I care to think about, I've been lectured, condemned, even told to go to hell on occasions by a beautiful, slim, gray-eyed witch. She became a part of my life to such an extent that I find I'm miserable without her."

Shannon looked away, but she could still feel him watching her. Somehow the crisp lecture she'd intended hadn't come off as she'd planned. When at last she ventured a look back at Cayce, it was to meet his sharp, slitted gaze—forceful, compelling, and ever watchful of her.

It was a battle of wills, Shannon convinced herself in that brief forging of their gazes. She was probably the first woman in Cayce's life to say no to an affair with him. Her brief lapse of the rigid rules where he was concerned had pointed out only too clearly that she wasn't capable of handling such an arrangement.

Cayce was such an overpowering individual, and Shannon was afraid of becoming absorbed within that aura of supercharged vitality surrounding him.

She'd fought too hard and too long for her own recognition to allow it to be ripped away by anyone.

"You say you want me, Cayce. Does this mean a ring, marriage, all the trappings that usually accompany such a proposal?"

"Like you, Shannon, I shy away from the binding ties of matrimony." A scowl darkened his face. "Marriage and its smothering confines are a sham. It winds up with two decent people snarling and growling at each other like two dogs. And God forbid if there happens to be a child born to the 'happy' lovebirds. It unwittingly becomes the bone between them." He stared into the colorless liquid in his glass. "That's not what I'm offering you."

"I see," Shannon softly murmured against the sting of his outburst. As she'd suspected, marriage was looked upon as a trap, nothing more. Cayce wanted, no, demanded, no strings in his relationship with a woman. He had no qualms whatsoever about using women.

It annoyed her that he could think her even remotely interested in such a relationship. "You do know that what you're suggesting is out of the question, don't you?"

"Why?" he asked brusquely. "What could be more enjoyable than two people who are compatible—and we are, Shannon, whether you care to admit it or not—to share a part of their lives with each other?"

The arrival of their dinner—thick, juicy steaks flanked by steaming baked potatoes—momentarily interrupted their heated debate. Shannon held her silence as the waiter placed the sizzling platter before her, then did the same for Cayce. As soon as they were alone, he resumed the conversation.

"I believe it's your turn," he remarked, his face unsmiling.

"You are correct. We are compatible, but where you shudder at the thought of belonging to one person, I think it would be wonderful . . . in the future, of course," Shannon informed him. "It would be wonderful to know I was loved by one man. I *do* believe two people can have a happy marriage." She paused, a tinge of sadness clouding her face. "My parents did. Their only problem was they should never have had a child. Their love for each other excluded everyone else, including me."

"Isn't this wonderful 'thing' you keep harping on what you thought you had with Jack Treen?" Cayce asked. "He didn't even wait till his ring was on your finger before he was unfaithful."

Shannon closed her mind to the callous reference to a part of her life that had been painful. "But that happened, mercifully, before marriage, Cayce. I was the one at fault for failing to see Jack for what he really was. As you so aptly pointed out, a schoolgirl crush can hardly be defined as true love."

There was a strained silence between them as each considered their next move. Shannon wasn't silly enough to dismiss Cayce as unimportant in her life. Even her long-awaited graduation and subsequent

136

position with the firm had been overshadowed by the realization that she wouldn't be seeing Cayce each day, wouldn't be called upon to sort out the inevitable confusion he always seemed to create on the eve of a trial. No longer would she be caught blushing from some blunt remark, a pointed reference to some part of her anatomy.

When he'd moved his office to Jacksonville—more a matter of relocation actually, the two towns being so close—she'd been secretly thrilled. But for what? Was Kitty correct? *Am I some sort of misfit who's afraid to risk any sort of involvement?* she asked herself. The questions kept coming, gnawing at Shannon's peace of mind, leaving her thoughts in a chaotic tangle. *No*, she raggedly admitted in silent acknowledgment, *I want to be with him; I want to have him touch me, make love to me, but I'm scared out of my mind.*

The admission was sobering, one she'd just as soon have kept submerged. She had an uncanny feeling Cayce could read her mind as easily as the menu they'd consulted earlier. That being the case, she knew she was treading on shaky ground.

"Having trouble accepting the inevitable, Shannon?" Cayce asked in his most casual manner, one which Shannon knew to be misleading. He was his sharpest when seeming to appear relaxed and calm.

"Are you asking out of concern or purely as a sense of amusement?" she murmured in a husky voice.

"Did you laugh when we made love, Shannon? Did you find it an amusing incident, knowing I'd bared my soul to you in that mindless moment of passion?"

"No," she huskily confessed. "I didn't laugh."

"Then please credit me at least that much sensitivity. I'm not looking to be amused by you. I can find amusement, and lots more, by simply making a telephone call." He shrugged one broad shoulder, a dark brow arching engagingly. "I will admit, I find your efforts to close me out amusing, but never you, Shannon," he softly countered.

"I want to practice law, Cayce. I don't want anything interfering with that."

"That's twice this evening you've accused me of having a disruptive influence in your life. Why is that, I wonder." His blue eyes danced merrily as he heard her now standard rejection of his proposal.

"Because you seem to be deaf when it comes to my refusing your . . . er . . . offer that we spend some time together."

"Correction. I'm asking you to make a commitment, Shannon. A commitment between a man and a woman for as long as you care to keep it."

She stared disbelievingly at him. Lord! He had more moves than a sidewinder! "Why do you avoid the correct terminolgy, Cayce? An affair is what you're suggesting, and it has been for some time."

"An affair, Shannon, is merely two people interested in satisfying their mutual sexual appetites," he lashed out in controlled fury. "Not only do I enjoy your body, but I find your mind to be stimulating as well. I enjoy discussing my cases with you; I value your opinion. There's only one part of you I would change."

"Oh?"

"Yes. Your damned barbed tongue. Someone should have turned you over a knee years ago."

Shannon couldn't help but smile at his disgruntled displeasure of her sharp criticism of him. Apparently he liked his women with less spirit than she'd shown, more easily molded to his way of thinking. "I'm afraid my grandmother is to blame. She was a very progressive lady, and encouraged me to speak my mind."

"I seriously doubt she intended you to devote your life exclusively to your career," he muttered scowlingly. He looked at her plate, then raised his eyes to glare at her. "You aren't eating. Are you deliberately trying to starve yourself to death? Isn't the steak cooked the way you like it?"

Instead of prolonging the darkness of his mood, Shannon hastily assured him that the food was excellently prepared. How could she say that he was the reason behind her loss of appetite? That when she was away from him he stayed in her thoughts. In his presence she was nervous, uncertain of herself. Either way she felt trapped.

CHAPTER EIGHT

The next week passed in a sort of well-ordered haze for Shannon. Each day was spent in assisting Josiah Hardwicke with the legal preparation of the Gore case.

She awoke in the mornings, accepted the glass of orange juice Kitty had waiting, sometimes grabbing a piece of toast, but more often than not, passed it by. Her arrival home, late in the evenings, followed much the same routine, with exhaustion sapping her appetite. A warm bath and bed were her only thought.

In the back of her mind she was well aware of the reason for pushing herself so. Aside from wanting to be well-prepared in court, she was attempting to expunge Cayce Hamilton from her thoughts and mind.

Contrary to her earlier fear that news of her supposed engagement to him would be a burning topic of conversation, she was surprised to find her colleagues' warm congratulations to be sincere and well-meaning.

Josiah Hardwicke appeared to be the most pleased of all, taking her slim hand in his own tissue-thin grasp and gently patting it. "I couldn't be happier, my dear. You and Cayce will make a fine pair . . . a fine pair."

His gentle praise reminded Shannon of a farmer extolling the merits of a matched pair of grays!

"Thank you, sir. Actually the news was a bit premature. We're both so busy, any sort of plans will have to be placed on hold." She hated herself for misleading the old gentleman. He was so sincere, she could have quite easily strangled Cayce for his part in the deception.

"I'm sure Cayce will put that situation to rights as soon as he returns from Miami. By the way, according to the media, he seems to be causing quite a stir. It's an interesting case."

"He usually does create a lot of excitement," Shannon said. She didn't bother to inform Josiah that she'd deliberately not been watching television or reading the newspapers. What would be the point of working herself to death trying to forget Cayce, then staring at his face on television?

The only person who knew the truth about Shannon's engagement to Cayce was Kitty. Knowing that a lengthy explanation would have to accompany the news, Shannon chose not to mention the matter during the frantic early-morning rush of getting to the office. Rather, she asked Kitty to meet her for lunch. Kitty had been away over the weekend, returning to the apartment long after Shannon was in bed and asleep.

Sure enough, Kitty was agog with excitement and curiosity after being informed of this latest development. Shannon endured the barrage of questions with tired calm, and then shocked her roommate by informing her that the story was a hoax.

"A hoax?" Kitty squealed in disbelief.

"Completely," Shannon replied in a flat voice. "Cayce walked in while Sam Jeffries was giving me a rough time about the Gore case. Before I could stop him, he'd threatened to rearrange Sam's face and informed my cowardly colleague that his harassment of, and I quote, my fiancée, should cease or else."

"That sly son of a gun." Kitty grinned like a Cheshire cat.

"Ha! Sly, my foot. Your boss is cooling his heels in Miami, while I'm left here receiving congratulations from all and sundry. For two cents I'd really spike his guns by announcing a date for our impending nuptials."

"You're really steamed about it, aren't you?" Kitty asked thoughtfully. "Why?"

"Because it wasn't necessary," Shannon bristled.

"He knew Sam would lose no time in spreading the news."

"Well, I for one can't see what you're so upset about. Of course, I don't share your views regarding Cayce. To me, he's a fantastic person."

"I know, Kitty, I know," Shannon replied tartly. "Have you ever considered having a go at him? I'm sure he'd be only too happy to oblige. You're probably the only woman on this side of fifty he's overlooked."

"Oh, my," Kitty laughed, not at all worried by Shannon's snide remarks. "I think the lady doth protest too much." A measured thoughtfulness was reflected in her twinkling eyes.

"Please," Shannon begged. "Spare me. At the moment I'm heartily sick of my fiancé."

On Friday evening Shannon called Kitty and informed her that she'd be working late again. Kitty pointed out in her harshest voice that unless Shannon wished to appear as a skeleton in her first dramatic moment in the courtroom, scaring holy hell out of the judge and jury, she'd better take time out for a quick sandwich.

"Get married, Kitty," Shannon yelled into the receiver. "You're mothering me to death! Who the hell cares if I look like a Halloween witch? It's my legal ability that will be watched, not my figure."

"In a pig's eye!" Kitty snorted. "Honest to God! I do believe you've flipped. I think I'll call Cayce.

Maybe he can stop this suicidal mission you've taken up."

"Mind your own business, Kitty," Shannon rapped out, only to find herself speaking into a dead line. Kitty had hung up on her. "Damn!" Shannon muttered, turning back to the work spread out on her desk.

She became absorbed in the case, losing all touch with time. The long hours of hard work were paying off, enabling her to see discrepancies in the story of the main witness for the prosecution. It would be tricky, but Shannon had the utmost faith in Josiah Hardwicke.

The first inkling she had that she wasn't alone came as Shannon bent to retrieve a piece of paper that fluttered to the floor.

A movement in her peripheral range registered at the exact same instant her fingers grasped the typewritten sheet. She turned her head, her paralyzed gaze seeing the expensive black handmade loafers, the dark gray trousers covering legs that seemed to go on forever.

She slowly straightened, resuming her upward study of her visitor over the top of the desk. When she encountered the icy blue of Cayce's steel gaze, she gave him a half smile. "You frightened me." Her voice was husky at the shock of seeing him.

"I'd like to do more than frighten you," he retorted as he walked over and stood before her, only the width of the desk separating them. He mercilessly

144

raked her with a cold stare. "Put it away." He indicated the work on her desk. "You're going home."

Shannon opened her mouth to argue and then stopped. Why not? She knew in her heart she wanted to go with him. Hadn't she nearly killed herself in order to free her mind of him? Escape the image of the face that haunted her?

Braving the severity of the icy blast he was subjecting her to, Shannon began gathering up the material, stacked it in a neat pile, then placed it in its folder and slipped a large rubber band around the bundle. She reached into the bottom drawer for her purse and rose to her feet.

"I'm ready." Her gaze was direct and uncluttered as it met Cayce's, the silent message that coursed between them needing no words, no explanation.

Once seated beside him in the car, Shannon turned and let her eyes rove the silhouette of Cayce's rigid features. There were signs of fatigue etched in the lines of his face, the tiny network of lines at the corners of his eyes more pronounced.

She wanted to reach out and smooth away the lines, erase the disapproving control that held him in its grip. Her hands clenched as she fought against this urge to make some sort of physical contact with the silent, brooding man beside her.

In the past she'd been witness to a number of moods reflected in Cayce's complex personality. Amused by some, angered by others. But this time was different, and she found herself nervous as she waited for some sign from him.

Shannon turned from the silent scrutiny to stare straight ahead. As she did she saw that they were headed in the opposite direction of her apartment.

Suddenly the strangeness of the moment, the silent rage emanating from Cayce became too much. "Where are you taking me?" The question was barely audible in the quietness of the car.

"To my place." Succinct and to the point! There was a determination in his tone that warned Shannon not to argue.

She sat back, letting her head rest against the luxurious velvet. Something or someone had upset Cayce to and beyond a point she'd never encountered. Did it have something to do with their supposed engagement? Shannon wondered as they sped by other cars, the orange glow from the streetlights casting an eerie reflection over the landscape. Was he just now beginning to realize the full implications of his carelessly spoken words? Was he beginning to feel the long-reaching tentacles of matrimony snaking toward him?

Shannon almost laughed out loud at the comical picture her mind conjured up, of Cayce shuddering in alarm at his impending doom.

"Is it a private joke or would you care to share it?" the subject of her thoughts said roughly.

"Private, and I've no wish to share," she told him saucily. "Exactly where do you live?" she asked after several moments went by. They were in a secluded area, where the homes sat well off the road, and were surrounded by trees and acreage.

"We're almost there," Cayce said stiffly, then turned onto a narrow black-topped road that seemed to disappear beneath a canopy of oaks. Approximately one mile farther the road merged with a concrete driveway, one section ending in a half-moon forecourt in front of a rambling house of modern design. The other section led to a three-car garage attached to the rear of the house.

Cayce brought the car to a halt on the apron in front of the garage and turned off the engine and the brilliant glare of the headlights.

Shannon turned to Cayce, who was intently studying her. "When did you buy this?"

"About a year ago. Why?"

She lifted her shoulders in a gesture of disbelief. "It's—it's not like you. I mean, I'd think an apartment would better serve your purposes." Her voice trailed off to a lame whisper.

"Oh, but think of the possibilities, Shannon," Cayce said smoothly. "An apartment limits me. Here"—he waved one huge hand encompassingly— "I can enjoy a weekend . . . a week . . . even months of such debauchery as to be mind-boggling. I can keep several innocent young girls at once sequestered from the prying eyes of neighbors, and gorge my depraved mind with the delights of their lovely bodies."

There was a flinty gleam in his wicked blue eyes as he looked at Shannon across the narrow space that separated them. The mockery in his face, the silent ridicule reminded her of times past when, in a similar mood, he would deliberately start a fight.

She calmly regarded him in return, never flinching as she watched the almost visible signs of him marshalling together his forces for a grand old battle! She raised her chin, thoughtfully running the tip of her thumbnail back and forth across the smooth skin.

"I think I've figured it out." She stared straight ahead in a contemplative pose.

"What?" Cayce asked, neatly stepping into the trap.

"There've been other occasions in our stormy relationship such as this. Times when you growled like a hurricane, snarling and lashing out at everyone in sight. It's just occurred to me that at each of those moments in your life you were between women." She turned her head and eyed him nastily. "You're the first man I've met whose personality is on a direct hookup with his libido!"

For one electric moment Shannon thought she'd gone too far. She felt rather than saw the large hand resting close to her shoulder clench, saw the grim tightening of Cayce's expression. "By God! That's ripped it," he stormed like a wounded bull, the hand now gripping her shoulder in a paralyzing grip.

"The hell it has!" she yelled in a voice just as loud, even if it did lack the same force. She reached up and knocked his hand from her shoulder, then slid around in the seat on her knees and faced him. "Now, you listen to me, you insufferable bastard!" Her eyes were like smoky velvet in their rage. "I'm tired and I'm hungry. Understand? I expect, no, I demand that you remedy the latter, and rather soon. The other I'll take care of myself when you return me to my apartment. I've no intention of filling in for your latest flame. Do you understand?" She sounded like a shrew.

"Er, if I didn't, I certainly do now," Cayce solemnly answered, only barely able to control the twitching at one corner of his lips. "May I say, Shannon, I never knew you to turn so violent when you were hungry. Does a steak sound tempting?" he asked as he opened the door of the car and got out.

"Fine," was her terse reply. She reached for her purse, her hand going for the handle, when the door opened. Cayce stood before her in gentlemanly fashion, one hand extended to assist her.

There was only the briefest hesitation before she let her hand be swallowed in his warm grasp. She ignored the surreptitious glances he kept sending her way as they walked to the back door.

Shannon stood to one side as Cayce unlocked the door, then reached around the doorframe and flipped on a light switch. He turned back to her, a grin on his face as he favored her with a sweeping bow. "Welcome, Shannon, to my humble home."

Humble indeed! Shannon thought a short while

later as she washed her hands and freshened her makeup in a sparkling blue and white bathroom, complete with an outrageously large sunken tub.

His housekeeper, who, Cayce had informed her, was away on vacation, was obviously of the old school when it came to cleanliness. Every part of the house Shannon had seen so far was absolutely sparkling from the efforts of the dear lady.

On her way back through the guest room that Cayce had put at her disposal, Shannon cast an appreciative eye over the uncluttered lines of the furniture, the draperies, and the carpet. The effect was pleasant and restful. Certainly not in harmony with the owner, she thought as she entered the hall and headed back to the kitchen and the tantalizing aroma wafting from within.

The sight that greeted her brought a grin to Shannon's lips. Cayce, with a large swath of material— she really couldn't call it an apron—tucked into the waistband of his trousers, was standing in front of the grill that was attached to the stove, carefully watching two thick steaks. On the counter she could see the beginnings of a salad, with two large Idahos baking in the microwave oven.

She studied the deft movements of his hands as he turned the meat. Was there no end to his talents? Just once she'd like to see him in a situation where he was totally at a loss. That mean thought gave an added sparkle to her eyes as she walked on into the room.

"May I help?" she asked in her most pleasing voice.

Cayce looked down at her, in spite of her high-heels, his gaze lingering on the softness of her lips. Shannon felt her body grow tense at this prolonged inspection, and shifted her feet uncertainly.

As if coming to some mysterious decision, he turned back to the steaks, his face an impassive mask that annoyed her. "You can finish the salad. The steaks need a few more minutes."

A soothing quiet hovered over the kitchen as they worked. Shannon could feel the tension slowly leaving her body, her appetite stirring for the first time in ages.

At some point during the past week she'd finally recognized that away from Cayce she was only half alive. She didn't like it, but there wasn't a whole lot she could do about it. Her battle against him had become a day-by-day effort, the outcome something she refused to think about.

Hard work, necessitating the application of all her thoughts and energies, got her through the daylight hours. But no amount of mental exercise, even fatigue, could stave off the memories of his touch. She knew she'd hidden behind a façade of disapproval, using it as a shield of protection. And yet part of her rigid condemnation had risen from a spark of jealousy that had steadily grown. She couldn't even remember when she first became aware of the humiliating emotion. It had taken root in her subconscious, blossoming into full maturity at a time in her life when it was most unwelcome.

The snap of tanned fingers before her face caused Shannon to jump, a startled squeak escaping her lips in surprise. "What was that for?" she cried, frowning, reaching for a dishcloth and wiping the juice of the tomato she'd been slicing from her hands.

"You were millions of miles away," Cayce drawled. He leaned one hip against the counter and stared at her, a smile easing the earlier grimness from his face. "You also eat as you slice." He reached out and flicked a tiny seed from her chin.

"I'll give you a larger portion of the salad," Shannon said pertly.

"Nothing doing. You're skinny as a damn rail now. I intend stuffing you."

"Really? What about me, don't I have any say in the matter?"

"No, Miss Priss," he retorted. "You have no say in the matter. I invested eighteen months in your career, and I mean to see my investment pay off. At the rate you're pushing yourself, you'll be burned out in six weeks."

Shannon kept her eyes riveted to the salad she began tossing, afraid that if she did look at him, he'd see how close to the truth he really was. She knew the pace she was keeping was quickly eating away at her body's reserves, but for the life of her, she couldn't stop.

There were so many things pushing her, so many

things she had to prove, so many things to forget. At times it was like being on a giant Ferris wheel that refused to stop, the constant motion leaving her dizzy.

Suddenly her wrists were gripped, stilling the movements of her hands. "Are you all right?" Cayce asked, concerned. "You've damn near worn out the salad." He took the wooden spoon and fork from her hands, then turned her around and gently pushed her toward the round table in the cozy breakfast nook. "Go sit down, I'll serve."

Contrary to his threat, Cayce wasn't required to utter a single word of encouragement. Shannon attacked her food with the gusto of a football player! Cayce, the faster eater of the two, in spite of Shannon's rejuvenated appetite, leaned back in his chair and watched her as she polished off the last bite of her steak and then reached for the remaining roll.

"May I get you something else, Shannon?" He pointedly eyed the lavish spread of butter she was applying to the roll. "Perhaps an apple pie? A quart of ice cream?"

"You, counselor, are a man incapable of being pleased. First you rant and rave about me being skinny. Now you gripe because I'm paying you the ultimate compliment by showing you that I enjoy your food. Make up your mind," she flippantly remarked, holding a portion of the roll before her mouth. "You can't have it both ways."

Cayce leaned forward and reached across the table

and caught her wrist. "I'll take you, you sassy wench, any way I can get you." He stared at her with a strange, flickering light in his eyes. Shannon sat motionless, unable to speak or move. "I'm not taking you home tonight, Shannon," he softly spoke, studying her face and the play of emotions that swept across it. "Kitty packed a bag for you, and you may consider yourself kidnapped for the weekend."

The piece of roll fell unheeded to her plate as the gist of what he'd said permeated the sense of well-being that had blanketed her. She pulled away from his touch and placed both hands in her lap. This was crazy. He wouldn't do anything so ridiculous. Besides, he knew she had the Gore case to work on. The trial started Tuesday.

"I'm afraid that as a comic, you don't measure up to your usual standard of excellence, Cayce!" The forced laugh that followed sounding just like that— forced. Surely he wasn't serious.

"You should know by now that I don't bluff, Shannon. So . . ." He rose to his formidable height and began stacking the dishes. "Why don't you go have a nice hot bath, while I pop these into the dishwasher. I'll have your suitcase in the bedroom before you're finished."

CHAPTER NINE

It was a bemused Shannon who, some thirty minutes later, found herself soaking in the sunken tub she'd earlier admired.

Her first thought after hearing of her outrageous abduction was to hurry to the bedroom in hopes of finding a telephone and calling a taxi. Her hopes were dashed, however, when she entered the room and discovered that if there had been a phone, it had been removed.

Out of curiosity Shannon walked over to the small table at the side of the bed and dropped to her knees. She pushed back the edge of the pale blue bedspread and stared at the round, cream-colored telephone jack, snug against the baseboard!

"The rat!" she muttered in a harsh undertone. "The stinking dirty rat!"

"Yes, Shannon?" Cayce spoke from the opened doorway. He walked over and placed her suitcase and smaller cosmetic case on the bed and then turned to observe her still-kneeling figure. "From the angry tone, I assume you've conjured up some additional grievance against me."

"You're damned right I have," Shannon hurled at him. "Why was the telephone removed from this room?"

Cayce heaved a huge sigh, one long forefinger going to the side of his nose as he considered her question. "Perhaps it was broken." He presented such an innocent face, Shannon was tempted to hit him.

"Try again," she snapped, her smooth brow creasing as she glared at him.

With an amused grin touching his lips, Cayce threw up his hands. "All right. You can stop snarling, Shannon. I unplugged the telephone so that you wouldn't be disturbed."

"And?"

"And so that you couldn't call a taxi and leave the minute my back was turned." When her dark look showed no sign of abating, he further explained. "I've been talking to Kitty every day, and she told me the state you were in," he grimly defended his stand. "I instructed her to pack enough clothes for you for a weekend and leave the rest to me. Now," he challenged her as he folded his arms across his broad chest, his feet spread apart, "are there any more questions?"

Shannon dropped her gaze and rose gracefully to her feet. She stalked over to the closet and stepped out of her shoes, then began fiddling with the difficult clasp of her watchband.

"No," she muttered, her fingers still working on the clasp of the watch.

Cayce walked purposefully toward her. He reached out and grasped her wrist, the catch opening under his superior strength. "You need a new one," he said, pocketing the oval gold watch that had been a gift from Jack.

"I like the old one," Shannon coolly informed him.

"Was it a gift?"

"Yes."

"From Treen?" he asked in a deep, harsh voice.

"Does it really matter?"

"It damn sure does to me. Was the watch a gift from Treen?" His eyes fixed on her face.

"Yes. But it was so long ago I hardly ever think about it."

Before she could move, Cayce's fingers were gripping her chin, forcing her to look at him. "Do you still think of him, Shannon?" he asked, a peculiar hoarseness in his voice.

For a brief moment she was tempted to taunt him by saying yes. She was still chafing from the dirty trick he'd pulled on her. But something held her back. The sobering realization occurred to her, as she stared into his eyes, that if she said yes, she would cause him pain.

"No, Cayce." Her voice was steady. "Not in the way you mean. And you're right, I do need a new watch."

The taut muscles in the rigid set of his jaw relaxed; that barely perceptible flicker of pain in his blue eyes vanished. His fingers slipped gently from her chin to steal over her shoulder and cup her nape. "Will you forgive me for deceiving you? I really was worried about you."

Shannon gave him a crooked grin, disarmed by the warm timbre of his voice. "I don't have much choice, do I? I'm not the sort to spend an entire weekend pouting. Besides, I'd rather have you wondering what I'll do to get back at you."

"Spoken like the true witch you really are," Cayce laughed. Before removing his hand, he tugged at the hairpins, not satisfied until her hair was tumbling about her shoulders in a silken mass. "That's better; wear it like that while we're here." He then brushed his lips against hers. "If you're not out of that tub in twenty minutes, I'm coming in after you," he threatened as he stepped around her and walked to the door.

With languid ease Shannon raised one slim leg from the nest of frothy bubbles and wiggled her toes. *It's amazing what a full stomach and a warm bath can do for a person,* she thought drowsily. It was unbelievable how she'd let even the simplest of physical comforts become mere objects of necessity. But she had. She also knew the reason . . . and so did Cayce.

So what do you do now, Shannon? that annoying little voice within her whispered. *Are you ready to be his woman? Ready to live for three months*—his affairs never lasted longer—*then return to the frozen shell you've existed in for so long?*

With a determined toss of her head, she willed her thoughts to other things. For no matter what she decided regarding Cayce, he would sweep her along, ignoring her protests without batting an eye.

Upon entering the living room, Shannon saw no sign of Cayce. She turned and started to the kitchen, when she happened to glance toward the large sliding glass doors that opened onto the patio and the swimming pool beyond. The glow from the light in the pool allowed her to see Cayce, seated on one of the sturdy redwood lounges, one arm behind his head, the other holding a drink.

Shannon quickly retraced her steps, the soft soles of her sandals muffling the sound of her approach. "For a moment I thought you'd deserted me," she remarked lightly as she joined him, seating herself on a matching lounge that had been drawn next to his.

He retrieved her drink from the tray sitting next to him on the table. He turned and handed it to her, his eyes running appreciatively over the light blue gauze blouse and the white silk slacks. "Are you sure you're warm enough?"

Shannon took the glass, murmuring her thanks. "I'm fine. I also happen to love this time of the year. Even though it's still early fall, there's a change in the way things smell, the lengthening shadows in the late afternoon."

"We'll go to New England next fall to see the foliage. Have you ever been?"

"Yes." She smiled at the thought of Cayce stamping about impatiently as she saw the beautiful colors.

"Did I say something amusing?" he asked scowlingly.

"No. It's just that somehow I can't picture you idling away your time by meandering throughout New England—or any other place for that matter."

"You really don't know me at all, do you, Shannon?" He watched her with that eagle-sharp gaze she'd seen so many times before. She shifted under the full brunt of his scrutiny, not at all sure how to answer.

"If you mean personal likes or dislikes—hobbies, then I suppose not," she honestly said.

"Are you afraid to delve deeper? Afraid that if you do, you'll find me to be a warm, breathing person after all?" He smiled at the look of chagrin that fluttered across her face.

"I wasn't aware that you welcomed someone prying and poking into your private life," she replied defensively. "Our relationship has been so stormy,

160

there hasn't been much room for the usual questions that normally occur between two people."

Cayce shrugged, neither angry nor disagreeing. "I know you, Shannon, possibly better than you know yourself."

"I doubt that." Her relaxed air began to fade. She didn't like the sound of this conversation. It was one thing to overlook the underhanded way in which he'd gotten her to his house; subjecting her to a tedious interrogation was another matter.

Cayce chuckled. "At the slightest reference to this feeling that exists between us, you become all prickly and angry. That intrigues me, Shannon."

"Practice your intriguing questions on someone else, Cayce," she sharply retorted. "I don't want to talk about it." She stared at the smoothness of the water in the pool and the reflection of the moon in its mirrored depths.

"I wonder why?" he retaliated almost thoughtfully, which Shannon knew from past experience meant I will know.

"Perhaps I've misjudged the depth of your feelings for Treen. You've said all along that you no longer love him. However, it's believed by some experts that a woman never forgets the first sexual interlude in her life nor the man involved."

Shannon slowly turned her head and stared at him, her body tensed, her expression one of annoyance. "Do you want me to do as you threatened once,

161

and rent a billboard? Proclaim to the world that I don't love Jack Treen?"

Cayce's dark brows arched significantly as he looked down the length of his nose at her. "Something like that." His tone of voice was deadly serious.

My God! Shannon thought wildly. *I'm not believing this.* She gave a slight shake of her head, as though to clear her thoughts. "You are beyond ridiculous, Cayce. You're insane. You've had enough women for ten men. Yet you sit there, chipping away at me about one single moment of youthful foolishness. At least I was acting under the assumption that the man loved me, that he was, and would be the only man in my life. What's your excuse?"

"It's different," Cayce grated, the icy glitter in his eyes leaving Shannon in no doubt as to his displeasure.

"Ah, so now we're finally learning that Cayce Hamilton really isn't in favor of equality between the sexes." She jumped on this diversion with both feet. "You know, you're rather like Sam Jeffries. You each have very definite ideas as to a woman's place. Well, I'm sorry to disappoint both of you, but I have a mind of my own, and I have no intention of being intimidated by your chauvinistic attitude." She swung her feet over the edge of the lounge and stood, glaring at his implacable features. "Good night!" she icily bid him, then stalked to her room, the glass held rigidly in her hand.

All the while she was jerking off her clothes, unmindful of their fragile quality, Shannon was silently cursing Cayce, damning him for his presence in her life, his chauvinistic attitude, for what he was, for making her love him.

She froze, her fingers releasing her blouse and letting it fall unheeded to the floor, as that last thought stood out in cold, stark reality. She loved him! She, Shannon Bankston, a level-headed, reasonably intelligent person, had fallen in love with Cayce Hamilton! A man who openly scorned every single thing she believed in. A man who was only capable of using a woman. He held back in each relationship, never allowing even the tiniest particle of himself to become involved.

Shannon stumbled over to the bed, clad only in beige-colored panties and bra, and sat down. She crossed her arms about her upper body as though warding off some horrible affliction that had slowly and irrevocably taken over her heart.

She thought back to the long months when she'd held Cayce off, realizing then the potential danger if she relaxed. Then had come the separation—the long months of adjustment without him. That same period had created in her a void, a hunger that grew in intensity until she was reunited with him.

Looking back, it became glaringly clear that her heart had been aware for ages what her mind had only now accepted. That accounted for the strange sense of unease that had settled over her when Kitty first arrived, and later, when Cayce appeared at her door.

Now, in painful retrospect, Shannon could see that a battalion of Russian Cossacks couldn't have stopped her from letting Cayce make love to her that night. For in her subconscious she'd been preparing for that moment since the first day she met him, the months of separation merely feeding the flames of her submerged desire for him.

With movements that were sluggish and clumsy, she pulled back the spread and sheet, and crawled beneath them, huddling in a fetal position against the shivering that was attacking her body.

Exhaustion combined with severe shock soon caused Shannon's lids to droop. She offered no resistance and drifted off to sleep. The only sign of her mental anguish being her tightly clenched fingers that were closed over the edge of the sheet, and the tiny trail left by an errant tear as it stole from beneath her lid and down her cheek.

Sometime later, still in the foggy mists of slumber, Shannon became aware of a delicious warmth that attached itself to her back, her hips . . even down the length of her thighs. She arched her body in a sensuous movement of contentment against the unknown pleasure and then became still again, her breathing relaxed and even.

But instead of returning to a sleep devoid of dreams, she seemed to be nestled in a cozy, warm space, made up entirely of Cayce. She could smell the clean scent of him, feel his hands warm on her body, the whisper of his voice in her ear, lulling her closer and closer.

Even his lips became a part of the dream as they nuzzled the soft, sleep-warmed skin of her neck, and caught the shell-pink tip of one ear and caressed it.

Shannon gloried in the spreading of desire that was slowly encompassing her entire body. It was so real . . . so real . . . And it seemed the most natural thing in the world to whisper her love for him, his own soft sigh of satisfaction bringing a gentle smile to her lips.

But suddenly she was caught up in a maddening confusion of half dream, half reality. Cayce's hands that had been gently teasing in their featherlike touch against her breasts now became more urgent, sending shivers of excitement to Shannon's mind, jolting her awake with her senses reeling.

"Cayce?" Shannon cried out in confused panic, only the outline of his head and shoulders visible in the darkness of the room as he rested on one elbow above her.

"Shh," he whispered against her hair as his hands smoothed away her fright, caressing her body in long, slow, sweeping motions. "Don't be frightened, darling, it's all right."

With the resolute swiftness of an arrow finding its mark, Shannon remembered the startling discovery she had made just prior to going to sleep, and the painful, almost unbearable realization of how wasted her love really was.

But instead of wrenching herself from her lover's arms—for he was truly that—she turned to him, opening her arms and drawing him against her womanly softness.

She brushed aside the momentary pangs of guilt at allowing Cayce to think she was still only half awake, using the cover of deceit to shield her desire for him, to cloak her vulnerability.

Like a thirsty nomad roaming the desert in search of water, and suddenly finding an oasis, Shannon became an impatient wanton on fire for this man who held her.

Instinct guided her hands to his head as she raised her lips to his, unashamedly the pursuer. The edge of her teeth nipped at the sensuous curve of Cayce's bottom lip, giving in to the primitive urge to exact a small measure of pain, not in retaliation, rather the necessity to communicate the depth of her passion.

Cayce's harshly indrawn gasp of pleasure merely intensified Shannon's appetite for him. She met the teasing foray of his tongue as it plunged into the heated softness of her mouth. She boldly defended his artful plundering and then surrendered to the overwhelming mastery and need of him.

The two flimsy barriers that prevented Cayce unhindered access to the silken body were dealt with, leaving him free to sample the perfection of each thrusting nipple that topped the creamy center of her breasts. He slowly seduced each tempting tip with his tongue, the warmth of his lips and mouth becoming a velvety soft enclosure that sent a direct shaft of awakening to the coil of desire that was fluttering in her stomach.

Shannon arched her body against the solid length of sinewy strength that was beckoning her, her own hands lazily caressing the broad shoulders before running over the smooth skin of his back. She was insatiable in her need to touch him, feel him. For too long she'd held back, afraid of letting Cayce know. But this once, she was throwing caution to the wind.

Her palms flattened against Cayce's broad chest, the thick, wiry growth creating an exciting friction. Slowly and deliberately her fingers touched and teased their way down to the taut, muscled flatness of Cayce's stomach.

A pleasured growl escaped his lips. He caught Shannon's hand and held it against him. "Don't stop, sweetheart, don't stop. I've never felt anything so beautiful as your hands stroking me," he whispered against her hair.

Shannon felt as though she were on a super-charged high, intent only on pleasing this man she loved. It was as though the startling realization had left her with a burning need to surround him with an affirmation of this love.

Cayce's breathing became tortured as his hands moved over Shannon's body in remembered ecstasy, his nimble fingers exploring the hidden secrets. Shannon offered no resistance, silently urging him on with a response that was more revealing than any words she could have spoken.

His lips started a tingling path that began with the crested tips of her breasts and continued downward until her entire body was a throbbing, quivering mass.

When he eased her onto her back and stretched his body over hers, Shannon lifted her hands and threaded her fingers through the dark thickness of his hair. At the gentlest touch against her knee, she opened her thighs to receive him, her slender legs intertwining with his hair-rough limbs.

"Oh, my sweet enchantress. How can I resist you?" Cayce whispered as his hands clasped her hips and raised them to meet the demanding force of his body. "You are mine, aren't you, Shannon?" He spoke harshly in the throes of passion. "Admit it. I want to hear you say it."

"Yes . . . yes," she cried out, matching the rhythm of his movements, soaring higher and higher with each powerful surge.

She was floating, falling, then soaring, each of the three phases of erotic sensations attacking her body with a rapidity that was staggering. The only steadying force in the swirling universe being the twin fetters of steel that clasped her to a solidness that was immovable, that carried her upward and into a world unlike any she'd ever known.

Their bodies blended in unison, merged into a mutual quest for pleasure that took them through the timelessness of space, the weightlessness of another plane. They were one, a beautiful and complete entity.

CHAPTER TEN

Shannon walked over and stared out the window of her office, knowing that in a very short while she and Josiah would be in the courtroom. The fingers of her right hand unconsciously twisted the unfamiliar feel of the large diamond solitaire on her left hand, her thoughts immediately taken over with the events of the past three days.

Cayce had given the ring to her after dinner on Saturday evening, their second night at his home. Shannon had protested furthering the pretense, but after one look at the stormy depths of his gaze, the hardened expression that swept over his face, she gave in. Her question of why had brought an unexpected answer.

"Let's just say I like the idea of your wearing my

brand, Shannon. It will give me some assurance when I return to Miami that you won't be going out with some other man. What with a number of people already knowing of our engagement, plus the fact that you aren't the type to remove my ring, I can breathe a little easier."

"Is that an off-handed way of saying you trust me?"

"Oh, yes, Shannon. You have no idea to what extent I've trusted you." This puzzling rejoinder brought a rush of questions, which Cayce effectively stemmed by placing a long forefinger against her lips.

"Just let it happen, Shannon. If you start now, that fertile imagination of yours will have created more problems in the next thirty minutes than I can work out in six months."

He brought both hands up to frame her face, the warmth of his gaze rushing over her like sunshine. "I will never hurt you, Shannon, never. Do you believe me?"

There wasn't the slightest hesitation in her answering nod. Too much had happened between them in the last few hours for her to think him capable of such a thing.

The doubts that were assailing her at the moment weren't directly related to Cayce. She knew that by having given her his ring, combined with that special pull between them, deceiving her was the last thing on his mind.

No, it wasn't Cayce, but her own thoughts, her

own doubts that were nagging at her. Because far from chasing him, as had been the usual case with most of the women in his life, Shannon now found herself in the enviable position of having been singled out by Cayce.

She found herself on the threshold of making a decision that, six months, even six weeks ago, would have been repugnant to her, that of preferring to live with a man rather than marrying him. Knowing Cayce as she did, she felt this was the only way she could hold him. And yet, his ring, his possessivness denoted a certain permanency that was in direct conflict with his previously expressed way of thinking. Shannon gave a slight shake of her head. It was baffling.

"Are you beginning to feel the noose tightening, sweetheart?" Cayce murmured softly, his hands slipping down to gently encircle her neck. "Let me assure you, the panic will gradually subside. I should know," he smiled. "I tried for six months to convince myself that you were satan's daughter, and that you were bent on destroying me."

"Were you successful?" she huskily asked, dreading yet wanting to hear his answer.

There was a rueful twist of his lips, his head cocked at a resigned angle as he stared down into her face. "I moved to Jacksonville, didn't I? A move, I might add, I'd sworn never to make. But I found myself afflicted with a strange malady, culminating in my having to be near a certain mean-tempered, disapproving young woman."

"You shouldn't have been so impetuous."

"Possibly. But I found the odds so much to my liking that I found I didn't want to bow out of the game."

"Lady luck doesn't always smile favorably on her subjects," Shannon added to the intriguing conversation. "And we both know what bad risks we are."

"But if I win, it will have been well worth the gamble."

They spent most of Sunday reviewing the Gore file, with Cayce going into detail regarding the complexities of the dying declaration that the prosecution was planning on using.

"In spite of the fact that Josiah is a wily old fox, and will probably do everything I've explained," Cayce said, "I want you to be aware of the procedure. It's not often used, and is one that is tricky as hell for the uninitiated."

By the time they reached her apartment late Sunday night, Shannon knew she would have stayed with Cayce if he had asked her.

If Cayce was aware of the unspoken surrender, he made no comment. He carried her bags in, checked out the apartment, then slipped an arm round Shannon's waist as she saw him to the door.

His kiss, while stirring and certainly arousing, wasn't nearly as long, as thorough, as ones in the past. Shannon watched him leave with a sense of dissatisfaction filling her. Her body was still adjusting to the high his lovemaking had aroused, and a simple almost perfunctory kiss did little to assuage the need within her.

Monday passed in a flurry of last-minute jitters for Shannon, with calm reassurances from Josiah. By the time she got home, she was ready to scream.

For once Kitty was a paragon of discretion. A quiet dinner, some television set the mood until Cayce called. After talking to him for a good thirty minutes, during which he kept the conversation on the Gore matter and the winding down of his own case, Shannon found herself as peeved as a wet hen.

"Not one word about missing me," she muttered to no one in particular as she slammed down the receiver. Her outburst caused Kitty to assume an extraordinary interest in the book she was reading, her grin of amusement hidden by the deliberate pursing of her lips.

After a few more minutes of watching television, Shannon bid her roommate good night in a disgruntled fashion, and stalked off to bed.

With a reluctance that puzzled her, Shannon forced herself back to the present. A quick glance at the small clock on her desk—a necessity since Cayce had taken her watch—showed that it was time to join Josiah in his office. She picked up her purse and briefcase, ran a smoothing hand over the collar of the white silk blouse she was wearing beneath the light gray suit, and headed for the door.

"I hope you haven't gotten your hopes up for a long trial," Josiah informed Shannon several minutes later as they walked from their offices to the court-house. "If my plan works, we should be out of there in about an hour and a half."

"I'm sure you'll be able to convince the judge, Mr. Hardwicke. Just as I'm sure I'd never have thought of the particular line of defense you've chosen. How-ever, you and Cayce seem to share the same views regarding the dying declaration."

"Well," Josiah began patiently. "It's risky, but I think it's a risk worth taking."

"How do you really feel? Do you think our client is guilty or innocent?" Shannon asked curiously.

"Personally I think the man is innocent. But re-gardless of personal opinions, my job is to provide him with the best defense available. One that will get him an acquittal or, as we hope, a dismissal of the charges against him. Never take a case unless you feel you can defend that person totally and complete-ly."

Which was exactly what Josiah Hardwicke did, Shannon later observed as she listened to him argue that though the deceased had been shot with a small caliber pistol, his death was a result of internal bleed-ing. The autopsy report bore out this theory, stating that upon entering the shoulder, the bullet struck a bone, deflected downward, and severed an artery. The victim had no way of knowing he was bleeding internally, and due to the smallness of the wound, wasn't overly concerned.

Josiah further stated that for the dying declaration to be admissible evidence, a doctor would have had to have told the victim he was dying. He further pointed out that since there were no witnesses to the crime, as well as the weapon never having been found, the charges against James Gore should be dropped.

The judge concurred, and the case was dismissed for lack of evidence.

Though winning in the courtroom was "old hat" for Josiah Hardwicke, Shannon's excitement at the outcome of the Gore matter was infectious. After conferring with their client, and seeing that relieved gentleman on his way, Josiah suggested lunch.

"I know it's a bit early, but I think we deserve a nice leisurely break."

It was sometime later, and they were lingering over a last cup of coffee. All while they ate, Josiah had kept Shannon laughing with amusing incidents from his years of practice. She'd found herself thoroughly entertained, and wondered again why he had never married.

During a break in his stories he looked past his assistant's shoulder. "I think we're about to have company."

"Oh?" Shannon murmured, then nearly croaked. For almost before the word was out of her mouth, they were joined by Jack Treen!

He stood by the table, smiling broadly. "Josiah, Shannon. That was brilliant strategy the two of you used in court, simply brilliant," he enthused. Though he lavished his praise equally, it was on Shannon that he kept his gaze turned, his eyes glowing at the serene beauty of her face.

"That's a very nice little speech, Jack," Josiah said. "Miss Bankston and I thought it would be simpler to allow our colleagues to stop and congratulate us here, rather than having the phones at the office tied up all afternoon."

"Very good, sir," Jack laughed condescendingly, "very good."

"Would you care to join us?" Josiah asked dryly, his shrewd eyes not missing Shannon's less than enthusiastic greeting to the younger man.

"Why, yes," Jack agreed. He pulled out a chair and sat down. "I've already eaten, but a cup of coffee would be nice." He turned back to Shannon. "How are you, Shannon? It's been almost a year since I last saw you."

"I'm fine." She offered nothing more than the two words. She knew she sounded inhospitable, but exchanging idle pleasantries with a person she detested was not an easy task for her.

"I understand you're no longer with Grady and Soames," Josiah casually remarked as the waiter set a cup and saucer before Jack, and then poured his coffee.

"No, I'm not," Jack said, somewhat embarrassed.

He named another firm he'd gone with, located in Miami. "Once Pamela and I decided on the divorce, it seemed best for all concerned for me to leave."

Ahh, Shannon thought, perking up at this bit of news. No Pamela, no cushy position in Daddy's firm. She also wondered if there was an unattached daughter tucked away among the musty tomes of the current firm he'd gone with.

"I'm sure it was a wise choice," Josiah said smoothly. "By the way, Miss Bankston is about to embark on the road of wedded bliss."

Shannon met his amused gaze and wondered if he was aware that she and Jack had once been engaged.

"Shannon?" Jack asked sharply. "You're engaged?"

"Yes. To Cayce Hamilton. We haven't set a definite date, but tentative plans are for sometime around Thanksgiving." She touched her napkin to her lips and looked at Jack. "I'm sorry to hear about you and Pamela." *And that's a bald-faced lie,* the tiny imp inside her whispered. *You couldn't care less about him or his marital problems.*

"I hate to break up this happy threesome," Josiah announced as he pushed back his chair. "But I have an appointment in twenty minutes. You stay and chat with Jack, Miss Bankston. I'll see you when you get back to the office." He shook hands with Jack, smiled at Shannon, and was gone.

Once they were alone, Jack turned back to Shannon, his gaze going to the ring she wore. Before she

178

was aware of his intentions, he reached across and caught her hand, drawing it toward the center of the table.

"It's beautiful, Shannon," he finally murmured, after studying the large diamond. "And I'm very happy for you." He raised his head and looked at her. "I only wish—"

Whatever he was about to say was abruptly interrupted by a large, tanned hand that seemed to come out of nowhere and disengaged Shannon's hand from Jack's grasp.

"Cayce!" Shannon cried, her eyes looking upward and meeting the flaming rage of his blue orbs. "I wasn't expecting you." She spoke unthinkingly. He was angrier than she'd ever seen him, and for the life of her, she couldn't think of a single thing to say to smooth over the awkward moment.

"I should think that's obvious," he snarled. "If I'd known you'd suddenly started taking long lunch hours, I would have gotten here sooner." Not by even the arching of a brow did he acknowledge Jack's presence.

By now Shannon had recovered from her initial shock at seeing him so unexpectantly, and was beginning to be angered by his boorish manners.

Just who did he think he was? What right did he have to humiliate her, especially in front of Jack?

"You do remember Jack, don't you, Cayce?" Her tone of voice, in spite of its honeyed tones, conveyed the anger she was feeling at being treated like an errant child. "Won't you join us?" she asked, smiling sweetly up at him, only the swirling storm in her gray eyes belying the courteous gesture.

"No, thanks," Cayce replied in a steely voice. "We have things to do. I suggest you say good-bye to Mr. Treen, and we'll be on our way." He hauled her to her feet as he spoke.

Short of stamping her foot and really causing a scene, Shannon had no choice but to go with him. She grabbed her purse and briefcase, and then looked at Jack, who was sitting as though carved from stone, with a faintly apologetic grin on her face.

"Good luck with your new firm, Jack," she said as Cayce began striding toward the exit, his hold on her wrist tightening.

As soon as they hit the street, Shannon turned on Cayce. "How dare you embarrass me like that," she hissed in an indignant undertone.

Cayce simply ignored her, continuing in his determined stride toward the parking lot. His face was a rigid mask of fury.

"How dare you haul me out of that restaurant like a disobedient child," Shannon continued to rage.

"You should be thankful I didn't do more than haul you out. I don't care at all to walk in and find my fiancée holding hands with an old flame," he said icily. He halted momentarily as he searched the parking area for the Mercedes, then forged ahead once again, dragging a sputtering Shannon in his wake.

"I wasn't holding his hand, you lumbering idiot," she exclaimed. "He was admiring my ring—that's all. Besides, Mr. Hardwicke had just left us. I really can't see what you're so steamed about, Cayce. I'd barely said half a dozen words to him when you showed up."

Cayce came to a halt beside his car, wrenched open the door, and bundled his recalcitrant fiancée into the passenger seat. By the time he was behind the wheel, Shannon was turned in her seat, ready to take up the issue again.

"You really are acting childish about this whole thing, Cayce," she loftily informed him.

Instead of continuing to exchange insults as she was wanting him to do, Cayce again ignored her. All his attention was focused on guiding the Mercedes from the parking lot and easing it into the line of traffic.

Shannon bristled at his cavalier treatment. She racked her brain for anything that might draw a reaction from him. He'd embarrassed her, and she wanted her revenge. "I do hope you realize that you were very rude to Jack. You didn't even speak to him." She then sat back and waited for the explosion. When it didn't come, she cast a surreptitious glance in Cayce's direction.

The only visible sign that her arrow of attack had hit its mark was in the extreme pallor of his face. Shannon was immediately contrite. Why on earth was she taunting him with references to Jack?

Because he feels betrayed, and you feel guilty for having been caught in what looked like a compromising situation, her conscience whispered. *You're also frightened of this new relationship and uncertain of the outcome.*

Shannon sat quietly for several minutes, no longer wanting to annoy Cayce, the love in her heart for the large, silent man at her side filling her with compassion for him and the obvious hurt he was suffering.

Before she could change her mind, she reached out and placed her hand on his arm. "I'm sorry, Cayce. I'm really not concerned that you didn't speak to Jack." She sighed. "In fact, I didn't act much better when he appeared at our table."

"Then you didn't meet him for lunch?" Cayce asked, never taking his eyes off the road. "Josiah really was there?"

"Until about five minutes before you arrived. We came directly from court. He was treating me to lunch because we won our case, rather, he won the case. We were on our last cup of coffee when Jack came over."

A shuddered sigh of relief made a soft, hissing noise as it passed through Cayce's lips. There was a slow but definite relaxing of his features. He turned his head and gave Shannon a short, quick look. "I've never experienced anything like that before, Shannon, and I don't mind telling you that I hope I never do again." He turned his attention back to his driving, but not before he caught her hand in his huge grasp.

By now Shannon knew their destination was Cayce's home on the outskirts of town. She wondered what Josiah would say to her playing truant, then promptly dismissed the thought. She had a feeling things were headed for a showdown between her and Cayce. One part of her was looking forward to such a thing happening, the other part wanting to run and hide.

Presently they left the highway and turned onto the private road that led to the sprawling house beyond.

When Cayce brought the car to a stop in front of the garage, Shannon opened her door and was already out before he could reach her. Without looking directly at him, she started toward the back door. "Is your housekeeper still away?"

"Yes, and she will be for the remainder of the month," Cayce told her. He held open the door for her and then followed her into the long, sunny kitchen.

Shannon, uncertain as to what to do, leaned against the counter, her palms braced against the surface on either side of her. She watched Cayce as he removed his tie and jacket. He walked toward the refrigerator, pausing when he drew even with her. "I believe this should be a suitable replacement." He placed a slim velvet box next to her right hand.

Shannon picked up the box and opened it, her gasp

of pleasure bringing a grin to Cayce's face. "It's beautiful, simply beautiful." The watch was round in shape, small, and surrounded by diamonds. The exquisite work of the band was so delicately done, Shannon was almost afraid to wear it. Sensing her hesitation, Cayce removed the watch and placed it on her arm, his large fingers remarkably deft as he fastened the tiny clasp.

"Thank you, Cayce," she whispered.

"You're welcome," he gruffly replied.

"Have you eaten?" Shannon asked.

"No." He gave her a lopsided grin. "I suddenly lost my appetite when I saw whom you were with."

"Let me fix you something," Shannon offered. She stepped around him and opened the door of the fridge. "Let's see, we have roast beef, chicken; there's also some ham. What will it be?"

"Roast beef sounds good," Cayce said. He moved over and leaned one broad shoulder against the wall, his tense, smoldering gaze never leaving Shannon as she moved about his kitchen.

"What do you want on your sandwich?" she asked, remembering from the weekend some of his particular likes and dislikes regarding his food.

"Mustard, dill pickles, mayo . . . Will you marry me?"

"Mustard, dill pickles, and mayo," Shannon repeated in an undertone as she removed the required ingredients from the fridge. "That sounds like a . . ." Her voice trailed off to a disbelieving whisper.

She shook her head as though to clear it. Had she heard correctly? Had he asked her to marry him?

"Yes, Shannon, you heard correctly. I did ask you to marry me," Cayce murmured softly across the width of the room. "The unprecedented tomcat of all times"—he smiled at the flush that stole over her face as he repeated the angry words she'd once flung at him—"has been declawed and put on a leash by a gray-eyed witch. She's woven her spell so completely, I'm helpless to escape."

Shannon stood silent amid this unexpected surprise, the calm serenity of her inner being, the happiness welling up within her, reflected on her face. Suddenly a smile touched her lips as she returned the warmth of Cayce's gaze.

"What are you smiling about?" he asked, still making no move to touch her, a controlled alertness about him.

"That's the first honorable proposal you've made me since I've known you."

"Never mind the correctness of the question or the lack of such regarding my past attempts on your virtue. What is your answer?" he growled.

"Aren't you going to allow me my rightful moments of indecision?" she teased, her heart singing.

"No," he rapped out. "Nor will I give you weeks or even days to plan a wedding. I want you with me every minute of the day, Shannon Bankston. I want your face to be the last thing I see at night and the first thing I see in the morning."

"What about love, Cayce? Is an expression of that small word a no-no?" she quietly asked.

A frown drew the dark brows together across the prominent bridge of his nose. "I love you," he said almost defensively. "That should be obvious."

"You certainly don't sound pleased about it," Shannon pointed out.

"I haven't noticed your being overly vocal on the subject."

"I do love you, Cayce. So much so, that I was going to tell you that I was ready to live with you. I want to be with you, too, anyway I can. Is that admission enough?" she asked.

"Oh, yes, my darling, it's more than enough." Cayce smiled. He held out his arms. "Come to me, Shannon." In a flash she was across the room and crushed against the solid wall of his chest. "Oh, God! I do love you," Cayce whispered against her hair. "So much so that I've been slowly going out of my mind for the last few months." His hands were running feverishly over her body, his lips raining kisses on her upturned face.

"I know," Shannon gasped between the light, teasing kisses. "It hasn't been pleasant for me either."

"You'll stay with me until we're married?" His arms tightened convulsively about her body.

"Yes. But there's one thing I won't do."

"What's that?"

"I've no intention of giving up my career. Does

that bother you?" Shannon asked. She placed her palms against his chest and met his gaze unflinchingly.

"There's only one way I'll ever want you to neglect your career," he said.

"Oh?"

"When you take time off to have our children. You do want children, don't you?"

"At least six," Shannon replied. "Think you can handle it?"

"With pleasure." He kissed her long and hard, then drew back and looked down at her. "I can think of a far more comfortable place for this remarkable conversation to be taking place than the kitchen."

"Oh?" Shannon asked throatily, her gray eyes glowing unashamedly.

"Yes," Cayce replied as he swept her off her feet and into his arms.

"Cayce! It's the middle of the day," she shrieked, correctly reading the determination in his blue eyes.

"How astute, sweetheart," he chuckled, never breaking stride till he entered the master bedroom. Once beside the king-size bed, he paused and stood her on her feet, his arms still around her.

"Was that a hint of disapproval I heard in your voice?" Cayce asked in mock sternness, his hands already easing the jacket of her gray suit from her shoulders.

"Of course not, counselor," Shannon replied in a

teasing manner. "It's just that I'm unacquainted with the ways of a rake. Love in the afternoon seems the perfect break. I'm sure I'll have no trouble falling in with your ways."

Her hands joined Cayce's in removing their clothing and soon the softness of the bed cushioned the fall of their bodies.

There was none of the haunting sadness in Shannon's eyes as she gave in to the warm gentleness of her lover's hands. She stared at the face that had become so dear to her, in her mind tracing the harsh lines of his features. She finally focused on his mouth, which she knew could be a weapon of seduction one minute, only to merge into a rigid slash of anger the next. Now the lips were tender, sensuous as they gave added pleasure to the embers of desire between them that he was urging into a flaming inferno.

With an openness that shined beautifully and directly into her eyes, Shannon opened her arms, silently beckoning Cayce to take her, make her his very own.

"No more regrets? No more doubts?" he whispered as he braced himself on his elbows above her.

"No," she quickly answered, pulling his head down and kissing him.

"Then the defense rests, princess."

Only the gentle shadows of the afternoon and the quietness of the sprawling house were witness to the man and woman as they made love. The silence was broken only by the harsh cry of fulfillment, and the softly murmured response.

Later, nestled in the protection of Cayce's arms, her head on his chest, Shannon exhaled a deep sigh.

"Happy?" he whispered against her forehead, idly twisting a long tendril of flaxen hair around one finger.

"Yes," Shannon whispered. "So much so that I'm afraid it's all a dream."

"It's not a dream, sweetheart, believe me. For my part, I've gone through hell to get you right where 'ou are," Cayce rasped.

Shannon raised herself up on one elbow, her face still glowing from their lovemaking. "You were very pushy," she informed Cayce.

"Do you mind?"

"I'll think about it," she grinned. "Somehow I can't see our marriage as all roses. We're both too stubborn to be bossed by each other."

"But think of the fun we'll have making up," Cayce whispered. "I can see it now. We'll work in the morning, argue at noon, make love in the afternoon, have dinner, and then make love again. How does that sound?"

"Oversexed!" Shannon tapped him sharply on the chin. "A condition I've suspected you to be suffering from for quite a while now."

"Speaking of our marriage, I've suddenly remembered a neighboring state where a couple can be married without delay. Would you like to take a short trip?"

"Certainly," she agreed, her face beaming.

"Well, then, the about-to-be Mrs. Hamilton. We'll stop by your place so that you can pack a bag, while I call Josiah Hardwicke and tell him that I'm absconding with his beautiful assistant."

"Somehow I don't think he'll be surprised."

"Of course not." Cayce eyed her devilishly. "I told him not to become attached to you when you first went to work for him."

"When I first . . ." Shannon spluttered. She stared at him, an outraged expression on her face. "You didn't!" she exclaimed, suddenly remembering how easily she'd gotten the position with such a prestigious firm.

"Not what you're thinking," Cayce countered in an equally strong voice. "All I did was inform Josiah how I felt about you, and that I intended to marry you."

"Is that really true? You didn't insist he hire me?" she asked, wanting to believe him.

"I would never have insulted you or your ability by asking him to hire or to keep you if you hadn't been capable of doing the job." He framed her face with his hands and stared deep into her eyes. "Do you believe me?"

"Yes," and she knew in her heart that she did. More surprising was the sense of pride she felt in knowing that even then, Cayce had been watching over her. Her eyes mirrored the deep love she felt for this man who had loved and protected her even when she'd been so doubtful of his every move. He was her life, her mainstay, and she never again wanted to be apart from him.

LOOK FOR NEXT MONTH'S
CANDLELIGHT ECSTASY ROMANCES ®